Longarm dove to the left as he saw a big man with a sawed-off shotgun come through the opening between the two rooms. The scattergun exploded, and Longarm fired with both hands at the gunner in the doorway. The heavy lead slugs from the scattergun blasted through the space where Longarm had been, thudding into the wall. The roar of the shotgun blast and the two six-gun shots filled the room with a rolling thunder.

The big man had been striding forward. The force of the two big lead slugs stopped his advance. He teetered on his feet a moment, then dropped the shotgun and crumpled to the floor with a round in his left lung and another through his nose. The head-shot slug had slanted upward into his brain and chopped up a dozen vital functions. He was dead before he hit the floor.

*   *   *

SPECIAL PREVIEW!
Turn to the back of this book for a special excerpt from the next exciting western by Giles Tippette . . .

Dead Man's Poker

. . .The riveting story of a former outlaw's biggest gamble, by America's new star of the classic western.
Available now from Jove Books!

DON'T MISS THESE
ALL-ACTION WESTERN SERIES
FROM THE BERKLEY PUBLISHING GROUP

THE GUNSMITH by J. R. Roberts
Clint Adams was a legend among lawmen, outlaws, and
ladies. They called him . . . the Gunsmith.

LONGARM by Tabor Evans
The popular long-running series about U.S. Deputy Marshal
Long—his life, his loves, his fight for justice.

LONE STAR by Wesley Ellis
The blazing adventures of Jessica Starbuck and the
martial arts master, Ki. Over eight million copies in print.

SLOCUM by Jake Logan
Today's longest-running action western. John Slocum
rides a deadly trail of hot blood and cold steel.

TABOR EVANS

LONGARM

AND THE TAOS TERROR

JOVE BOOKS, NEW YORK

LONGARM AND THE TAOS TERROR

A Jove Book / published by arrangement with
the author

PRINTING HISTORY
Jove edition / February 1993

ISBN: 0-515-11043-4

Jove Books are published by The Berkley Publishing Group,
200 Madison Avenue, New York, New York 10016.
The name "JOVE" and the "J" logo
are trademarks belonging to Jove Publications, Inc.

PRINTED IN THE UNITED STATES OF AMERICA

10 9 8 7 6 5 4 3 2 1

Chapter 1

Custis Long felt remarkably well this Monday morning as he marched down the street on his way to take a new assignment. A week of shuffling Billy Vail's paper had quickly proved to be more than he could tolerate. He dropped two cents into the outstretched hand of a newsboy, picked up his *Rocky Mountain News,* and swept around the corner of Cherokee and Colfax in Denver, Colorado.

He walked up the hill toward the Federal Building. Custis Long, known over much of the West as Longarm, was lean and lantern-jawed. His full, longhorn moustache spread wide and curled slightly upward at the ends. His rawboned features had cured saddle brown from his time in the wind and the sun. Longarm's gunmetal blue-gray eyes stared at life with a knowing smile in them. His tobacco-leaf-colored hair curled slightly, showing under his flat-topped, snuff-brown Stetson.

At the Federal Building, he strode inside, mounted the marble staircase, and pushed through an oak door with gold-leaf lettering that indicated this was the office of Billy Vail, United States Marshal, First District Court of Colorado.

"Morning," Longarm said to Henry, Billy's prissy-looking clerk, who was huddled behind his clean desk. The young man looked up and waved, so Custis moved on through the room and into Billy Vail's private office without knocking.

"Damn! You did it again," the United States marshal, appointed by the president, said as he slammed the bottom drawer shut, covering his private stock of sipping beverages.

Longarm slid into a red Morocco-leather armchair and glanced up at the banjo clock on the wall. He was only fifteen minutes late. Not bad.

U.S. Marshal Billy Vail ignored Longarm for a moment and lifted a shot of whiskey to his lips. He downed it in one gulp, sucked in a breath of cold air to put out the throat fire, then gave a short sigh and put down the glass. Billy Vail ran one hand back over his balding head, and his naturally pinkish complexion turned even redder.

Longarm was ready for the usual chewing out about being late to an appointment, but surprisingly, Billy didn't even glare at him.

"We've got a problem, Long, and you're the one who has to get it straightened out, damn fast!"

"Problem, Boss?"

Billy flipped him a file that held several sheets of paper.

"It's all in there, carefully typed by Henry so you can read it. Briefly, we had a bank failure here eight years ago. Man by the name of Wallace H. Johnson had a bank that went belly-up to the vultures. His top vice president, one Ira Casper, embezzled fifty thousand dollars and vanished, and the bank went under.

"Six months later, Johnson was so torn by shame, fury, and depression that he took his own life. He couldn't stand to meet friends of his who were now paupers because they'd lost everything when his bank failed. He blamed himself."

"That's why I ain't never trusted banks," Longarm said. He pulled a brown cheroot from his pocket, nipped off the end, wet the outer leaf with his tongue, and lit the tobacco with a match. Billy Vail watched him, frowning at the cloud of blue smoke, then went on.

"Friday I got a wire from the president, along with orders from the Justice Department that I was to make the Johnson-Casper matter my top priority and get it cleaned up as fast as possible. Turns out the president was an old school friend of Johnson senior.

"The president said to take care of the problem at once. Seems the son of Johnson, Wallace H. Johnson, Jr., is now in

2

Taos, New Mexico, where he claims he has found this Casper, the man who embezzled the money from his father's bank. He doesn't trust the law in Taos, and he wants a U.S. deputy marshal to rush over there and arrest the man and bring him to court here for trial."

"Sounds simple enough. When do I leave?"

"Last night if possible. Get over there, nail down this scoundrel, and bring him back here as fast as possible. I don't like having my boss and the president of the United States taking me to task. Get it done, pronto!"

Longarm stepped off the Conestoga stage from Santa Fe in the village of Taos, New Mexico Territory, at noon. He registered at the town's best-looking hotel, the Broadmoor, and asked the clerk where he might find Wallace Johnson.

The clerk looked about forty, with red cheeks, spectacles worn low on his nose, and a pair of cautious green eyes. "Oh, he's a guest here all right, but I heard he was in an accident this morning and died. Out on the north trail about three miles. The sheriff is still out there investigating."

Longarm dumped his gear in his room, rented a horse and saddle from the livery, and got directions to the site of the crash.

A half dozen horses stood on the trail near a cliff when Longarm rode up. He left his mount ground tied and stared down the void. It was a sheer fall for fifty feet, then eased into a steep slope over rocks and boulders to a line of green piñon pines and a sprinkling of taller ponderosa another seventy-five feet below.

The buggy and horse sprawled at the bottom over a hundred feet from the trail. Three men stood around a body smashed on the rocks, evidently where it had fallen from the buggy. The body, now only a splash of blue and red, lay at the bottom of the straight drop, fifty or sixty feet from the remains of the shattered buggy and the dead horse.

Longarm worked his way to the north around the sheer drop and down to the slope. Once there he walked ahead to where the three men stood near the body.

They looked up as he approached. He introduced himself as Deputy U.S. Marshal Custis Long, and the oldest man relaxed. He held out his hand.

3

"Yeah, the famous Longarm of the law. Heard a lot about you. I'm sheriff of Taos County, Nathan Murdock. I'm pleased to have you here. What do you make of this? An accident?" The sheriff was at least sixty and stooped a bit, with gray hair under a town hat and brown town shoes. He squinted at Longarm as he asked the question.

"Accident? Might be. Let me look around a little. Is this Wallace Johnson?"

"It is, or was," one of the other men said. He nodded but didn't offer his hand.

The third man looked at Longarm steadily. "I'm Dr. Amos Smith. Somebody figured I might be able to help Johnson here, but no surgeon in the land could bring him back. I'll be heading to town, Sheriff." The sawbones turned and walked away. The medical man was tall and slender, with intense brown eyes and a slight limp to his walk.

Longarm stared at the body. It lay facedown against a boulder. Johnson's split-open head could have caused his death. The rest of the crumpled body showed the effect of several broken bones in the sprawled, unnatural positions of the limbs. Only a little dried brown blood stained the rock.

"Johnson must have jumped out or fallen out of the buggy here when it came over the side," Sheriff Murdock said. Longarm nodded and scrambled down the steep slope to where the smashed buggy rested. The dun horse had broken free of the leathers and lay crumpled a dozen feet beyond the buggy.

Longarm looked over the wreck. It had been battered into junk by the fall. No sense in pulling it back to the road. He found the smashed buggy seat and frowned. The seat was sticky with what looked like red, half-dried blood. He bent and touched it, then smelled his finger. Blood for sure.

Maybe it was from the horse. The animal must have died quickly, because there was little blood on it. Longarm checked over the animal and found eight gashes that had not bled at all. That reminded him that a body doesn't bleed after the heart stops. There's no pump to continue pushing the fluid out of a wound.

So how did all that blood get on the buggy seat? He checked the horse again. Most horses are well aware of a narrow trail and tend to shy away from a drop-off such as this. Why did the animal go over the side?

4

He looked at the horse's head. One tear mark showed just behind the right eye, but it must have come from the fall. It had not bled at all. Longarm grabbed the bit and tugged and pulled and turned the horse's head so he could see the other side.

In back of the left eye he saw a burned, black circle in the horsehair, two inches in diameter. He looked closer. In the middle of the circle was a small, almost closed hole.

Powder burns. The animal had been shot from two or three inches away, just far enough to leave a strong burn. The horse had been shot; then it fell or was pushed over the side.

Longarm walked back up to Johnson's body. Two men had tied a rope under the corpse's arms and waited to drag it up the slope to the roadway.

"Everybody in my county gets a decent burial," Sheriff Murdock said.

The body had been moved, and now the head slid off the rock and rolled back. Longarm stared at the smashed-in side of the head and face. He looked at Johnson's throat. It was caked with blood. Why a bloody throat if Johnson died from a head wound?

Longarm lifted Johnson's head and probed at the throat with his kerchief. Chunks of dried blood fell away, and then Longarm saw what he'd been afraid he might. The gash of a knife blade showed across Johnson's pale white throat and left carotid artery. That's where all the blood had come from.

Wallace Johnson had not died in the fall. He'd been dead before he left the bank above.

Sheriff Murdock knelt beside Longarm. "I see it, son. I see it. Poor bastard died of a slit throat, not from the fall."

"Sheriff, the horse was shot in the head, leaving powder burns. Johnson was killed up on top and bled all over the buggy seat. Then the killer pushed the rig and the horse over the side.

"Sheriff Murdock, what we've got here is murder, not an accident. It was a planned, cold-blooded killing."

At the sheriff's signal, the three men above pulled on the rope, and one man followed the body up the slope to keep it from snagging on rocks. Longarm and the sheriff walked around the cold blue granite cliff and climbed up to the road. Sheriff Murdock wheezed and stopped to rest before they got to the North Road. Longarm guessed he was well over sixty-five years old.

5

When the sheriff caught his breath, he mounted his horse and they all rode back toward town. The body lay head-down over the saddle of a pack mule.

"So why are you in town, Marshal Longarm? Not to help me with this killing."

"In a way, Sheriff. I came to see Wallace Johnson. He had something important to tell me."

The sheriff looked up quickly. "Too damn bad, Longarm. Looks like he won't be able to tell you a thing now."

Back in town, Longarm cleaned up, then went for a late noon meal at a small café across from the hotel.

He had just sat down and ordered when a black-haired woman walked up and stopped in front of his table. When he looked up, he saw that she was dark and had the features of an Indian woman, an extremely pretty one. Her black hair was cut short, and she stared down at him with worry and concern. She wore a white blouse and a brown skirt.

"Pardon me, but I just saw you ride back to town with Sheriff Murdock. Is it true what people are saying?"

Longarm had stood as soon as she began to talk. When she finished, he frowned. "Miss, is what true?"

"About Wallace Johnson. Is he . . . Is he dead?"

Longarm held a chair for her and urged her to sit down. When she had, he sat across from her. "Yes, I'm afraid it is true. His buggy went over the side of a cliff."

Tears welled up in her eyes, and she let them come, crying softly. She took a white napkin from the table and blotted her face.

"I'm sorry. Did you know him?"

She nodded. "Yes. Oh, yes, I knew him. He'd been here only two months, but we were good friends. He said he wanted to stay here and . . . and be with me."

"Miss, my name is Long, Deputy United States Marshal Custis Long from Denver. I came to Taos to see Mr. Johnson. He wrote a letter saying he knew something and wanted to tell me. Would you by any chance know what he wanted to say?"

Her eyes widened. Then she shook her head. "Oh, I don't think so. Wallace said he was a detective here on a case, trying to identify someone. One day he was happy and pleased and said he'd found his man, but he wouldn't tell me what it was

6

about or the name of the man. That afternoon he sent four telegrams. He was excited and said at long last he would get some justice. He took me out to a big dinner that night and then to a traveling acting troupe's play."

"But he didn't tell you the name of the man he had identified?"

"No. About a week later he said he'd play a little game with me. He'd give me three sets of clues. If I could figure them out, then I'd know the man he'd come to town to find."

Longarm sat up straighter. "Three sets of clues. Did you figure them out?"

"I think I did the first one. I can show them to you if you want me to. Anything to help you do what Wallace wanted done. I . . . I loved him, Mr. Long."

He told her about the embezzlement case and that the man Wallace sought was probably Ira Casper, the embezzler. She nodded.

"Oh, let me introduce myself. I'm Jennifer Walking Dove. Yes, I'm a full-blooded Pueblo Indian. My parents died when I was young, and my grandfather sent me to school with the sisters in Santa Fe. Now I teach the white and Mexican children here in Taos. I know that's unusual, but they had trouble getting a teacher to stay and I told them I'd stay. I've been teaching here two years. I'm good at it. But this is June, so I'm out of school for the summer."

Longarm nodded, making sure to watch her, make eye contact, so she would know he was interested. Now, with Johnson dead, she might be the only way he could find out who Johnson had pinpointed as the embezzler.

"Miss Walking Dove, have you had dinner? Would you like to order something?"

"Oh, no, I . . . Well, I did miss a noon meal. I was so worried. Yes, would you mind?"

"I'd be delighted and honored."

A short time later she worked steadily on a roast beef dinner and Longarm grinned.

"You were hungry."

"Yes. Oh, I can pay for it."

He laughed softly and shook his head. "No, Miss Walking Dove, it's my treat. Besides, I want you to help me. Could

7

you show me those clues that Wallace left you?"

She looked up, her dark eyes black pools, her short hair framing her pretty face, and her mouth tight for a moment before it relaxed. Jennifer had a good figure, slender, and he guessed she was not over twenty-two or twenty-three years old. He noticed how pleasantly filled her white blouse was. She took a deep breath and Longarm grinned.

"Mr. Long, I'll be glad to show you the sets of clues that Wallace left, but only with the understanding that I get to help you find out what happened. I truly don't believe that Wallace would let his buggy go over a cliff."

Longarm nodded and they finished eating. When the dishes had been cleared away, he told her that Wallace had been murdered. It would be all over town within minutes, and he wanted to be the one to tell her.

The tears came, huge splashing ones that surprised him. She cried almost silently, watching him with first anger, then a resignation and understanding.

She took out her small blue handkerchief and wiped her eyes, then put it away. "I'm sorry. Sometimes I cry, not often. But I don't lose a person I love and respect often. Now more than ever I want to help you find whoever it is who killed Wallace."

"It's probably the same man who is the embezzler," Longarm said. "If we find one, we have them both."

"Yes. The clues. I should show them to you. The sooner we find him the better. Are you ready to go?"

She stood and so did Longarm. He paid the bill and she hurried him outside. They walked through the street to the near end of town, and she turned him away from the main avenue, angling toward a small white house set apart from the others on the street.

"This is the schoolmarm's house," she told him. "The district furnishes the house so they don't have to pay much salary. I also have two rooms out at the pueblo, where I lived before I went to the mission school."

They walked in the front door, which was unlocked, and Longarm frowned. Three wooden chairs, a table, and a small couch made up the total of sparse living-room furniture. The school board must have brought her the discards from its members.

Longarm furrowed his brow and touched her shoulder. "Jennifer, will people talk? I mean, should I be here with you alone?"

"Reality, Mr. Long. I'm an Indian. They expect me to steal and to cheat and to be immoral, by their standards. It doesn't matter. They have signed a contract for the next school year with me. Anyway, it's my life to live the way I wish to. Now, let me show you the clues."

She took out a large brown paper envelope and opened it. From it she withdrew three small packets of papers. Each one was fastened with a clothespin.

"Here they are. He said I had to work on the first one and that might help me with the second one." Jennifer spread out the items from the first bundle.

There was a one-dollar bill and a key cut out of cardboard. Other items included a picture of George Washington, a copper penny, a small medicine bottle with a label naming it "Itch Cream," a picture of a derby hat cut from a magazine, and a long key with T-15 stamped on it.

She spread them all on the table, leaving them in no order.

"You say you've figured this one out, but let me look over what he left and that might give me an idea how he thinks and make the second clue easier for me to decipher."

Longarm put the two keys together, then the dollar bill and the copper penny. Sitting alone were the itch cream, the picture of the derby hat, and the picture of Washington.

He stared at them for a while, then took the picture of George Washington and put it with the dollar bill and the copper penny.

"Why did you put George Washington's picture next to the dollar bill?"

"Money, the bill and coin are money. George Washington's face appears on many of our coins, that's money. It could be a tie."

He looked at what was left. Then he picked up the long key and examined it. He grinned and pushed it up into the row with the coins and the bill.

"More about money. That's almost exactly like a safe box key I have for my box at the bank in Denver. They're getting quite common now. Some call them safe deposit boxes. Again this is talking about banks and money."

9

Longarm stared at the paper key, the itch cream, and the derby hat. "Does anyone in town wear a derby hat like this one?"

Jennifer shook her head. "Not that I've ever seen."

"A derby hat to me talks about a man with money, a man of means." He put the picture of the derby up with the money and other pictures. "Now, that leaves us the dang blasted itch cream and the paper key.

"I'd have to think that the paper key goes above all the rest. It's saying, 'Here's the key to finding this man.' Then we find it among the clues he's left us. Which leaves the only other clue, the one that doesn't fit anything, the blue jar of itch cream."

Longarm stared at the clues again. Jennifer hurried over to the wood-burning kitchen range, built a fire, and put coffee on to boil.

"I figure that you're going to need a cup of coffee before you figure this one out," Jennifer told him.

He looked up and nodded but didn't hear what she said. He ran over again a theory that might or might not be right. He tried it on again. Itch cream. It didn't seem to fit. But it could if you thought of it not as a literal clue but as a kind of a sound clue.

What other words did people use to indicate a person with money? Of unlimited means, one of the elite, a rich man. Longarm paused. Rich . . . itch . . . The two words were so much alike that it stopped him for a moment. Yes. That had to be it. He moved the blue itch cream jar up in line with the others.

"Got it," he said.

Jennifer came over quickly, disbelief evident on her face.

"No, not so fast. It took me a week to figure it out. What does it mean?"

"All of the clues point to someone with money, or money itself, or someone who dresses elegantly as with the derby. The itch cream was the topper. Itch is close to rich, and I think that's it. Our embezzler, the real Ira Casper, is a rich man who lives right here in Taos."

She smiled, reached up, and kissed his cheek. "That's your prize for getting the first clue right. The next one isn't so easy. I've been trying to solve it for over two weeks now.

Wallace said he wouldn't help me with them, and he didn't. Now, let's have some coffee and then we'll start on the second clue."

Longarm sat at the small kitchen table where the clues had been spread and watched her pour the coffee, black, hot, and strong. He nodded.

"You make a good cup of Arbuckle."

"Lots of practice. I learned to like it at school. Few of my family and friends in the pueblos drink coffee."

"Probably better for them. Are you gonna give me a guided tour of the pueblos? I've seen them at various times, but always like to have a tour."

"Anytime you'd like—just as soon as we find out who killed Wallace." She watched him closely. "You are going to track down his killer, aren't you?"

Longarm hesitated. "That's not exactly my first responsibility here. It's a local problem. The trouble is I'm not sure that Sheriff Murdock will be able to do it."

Jennifer came around the table to where he sat, spread his knees, knelt between them, and reached up. Her lips met his and they were on fire. The kiss scorched his lips.

When she came away, she barely broke contact, staying close. "Custis, I truly want you to find the killer. I would have married Wallace if he hadn't been murdered. I owe it to him to trace his killer and see that he's punished." She unbuttoned two of the fasteners on her white blouse.

"Custis, I'll do anything you want me to do, so you'll find the murderer."

He watched her open the other buttons, and when she finished, she pushed the blouse back to each side showing her full, naked, pink-tipped breasts.

"Anything you want, Custis, now and in the days ahead." She stood and caught his hand. "Come on, let's not waste this time we have together."

He stood and stopped her, bent and kissed her breasts, then covered them with her blouse, fastened the top button, and worked down.

"Beautiful Jennifer. Nothing I'd rather do than take you into your bedroom. But right now we need to get back on the trail of Wallace's killer. Now is the most important time, before people forget or get their memories changed. We have to check the livery first and see when Wallace hired that rig. He didn't own one, did he?"

"No, he didn't own a buggy." She frowned for a moment, then sighed. "Yes, you're right. I do think you're the finest man I've met in a long time, and whenever I can do anything for you ..."

She straightened her white blouse, tucked it in her skirt, and brushed at her straight black hair.

"If you're finished with your coffee, maybe we'd better go down to the livery. I know most everyone in town."

The liveryman turned out to be the same one Longarm had rented his mount from earlier. He squinted when he saw Jennifer beside the stranger.

"Howdy, Miss Jennifer. You come to teach me how to spell?"

"I'm afraid that's a job too big for me, Scooter. Mr. Long here has a question for you."

Scooter looked as slow as maple syrup in a snowbank. He seemed to be near sixty but probably had used up no more than forty years of life. Half his teeth were missing; his dirty, gray hair hung long around his neck; and his full, salt-and-pepper beard held bits of straw. From bloodshot eyes, he looked up at Longarm.

"I'm interested to know when Wallace Johnson rented the buggy last night," Longarm said. "Early in the evening or midday?"

"Don't rightly recollect there, Mr. Long."

"You were working yesterday and last night, right?"

"Yep, near as I can remember."

Longarm grabbed the man by his shirtfront, lifted him to his toes, and pushed him against a feed box.

"Scooter, you better get your memory working better than that, or you won't have a need to remember anything."

Scooter's red eyes bulged and his face went white. He looked around frantically as if trying to find help.

"What ... what was that again?"

"When did you rent the buggy to Mr. Johnson?"

"Long about five o'clock. Yep, about five 'cause three guys came in on lathered horses just after that. Yes, sir, Mr. Long. About five o'clock."

"Thanks, Scooter. Always a pleasure talking with you."

The deputy marshal and the Indian beauty turned and strolled back toward Main Street.

They were almost there when two men ran past them holding pine branches over their privates. They were naked. Both men were smeared with colors—bright oranges, reds, greens, and browns.

"Would you look at that!" Jennifer said, then giggled. "I do believe those two gentlemen were in the altogether."

By the time Longarm and Jennifer got to Main Street there was a crowd around the two men. They both had on long shirts now to cover themselves.

" . . . so we did what they said," one of the half-naked men screeched. "Hell, they had guns and bows and arrows. Damned savages stripped us and painted us and booted us off the place we was working. Damn, we just doing what we was hired to do."

Longarm looked at Jennifer, who had uttered a small cry.

"Oh, no, those colors look familiar. We've got to find out what's going on here, right fast."

Chapter 2

Jennifer Walking Dove stared at the bright colors splashed on the two white men and groaned.

"I've been afraid this would happen," she wailed. "Let's get closer and find out for sure."

The two of them worked to the front of the crowd, and she called to the painted men.

"Where were you working when the Indians attacked you?" Jennifer shouted.

"Where? Down there by them humps in the ground just across the river, where Mr. Hamilton is putting up his new house."

The sheriff walked out of his office, his knees still stiff from sitting down most of the time since he got back from the cliff. He told the men to lead him to where they had been working.

Jennifer pulled Longarm's hand. "Down this way. I know where they're going. I've been worried about those mounds for a long time. If we run, we can beat the rest of them there."

They ran. They jogged over a block then headed for the river, the headwaters of the mighty Rio Grande that flowed right beside the town. Jennifer paused as soon as she could see the area she was looking for. It was across the river, and Longarm spotted a mass of Indians there in war dress, each one with a rifle or a bow and arrow. In the midst of them, they had built a typical Pueblo Indian burial platform. It was three feet off the ground, supported by cut poles, and tied together with strips of rawhide.

They ran faster. Jennifer told Longarm to stay on this side of the stream. She let go of his hand, splashed through the six-inch-deep water in the shallow creek, and ran up to the warriors. She questioned them quickly, and a moment later an older man came out of the group and she talked with him.

By then half a dozen white and Mexican men and women had straggled up to the bank of the river. The Indians came forward and motioned that no one should cross the water.

Jennifer stood on the far side, beside the old Pueblo man who Longarm decided must be the chief of the tribe. When the old chief saw Sheriff Murdock, he held up his hand for silence, and even the talking white and Mexican people quieted.

He motioned to the platform made of branches and on which were hung many feathers and skins of small animals, a bow and arrow, a lance, and other weapons and tools that the warrior-farmer used in his everyday life.

The old chief spoke in a loud voice in the tongue of his people. Jennifer Walking Dove translated his words.

"Two white men have violated Pueblo sacred ground. On this ground are buried the chiefs of the Pueblo nation for the last fifteen generations. The men who violated the sacred burial grounds should have been put to death. It is Pueblo law. But we are learning to live in peace with the white men. That is why we only painted them and sent them running.

"All of this area around the mounds is sacred land where no white man should walk. It is an insult to the dignity of our ancestors to have white men walk here.

"This land will be guarded and protected by Pueblo warriors. You have been warned. No white man may come across the river here or walk on the sacred monuments to our great chiefs. I, Running Fox, chief of all the Pueblos, have spoken."

By this time more than a hundred white and Mexican men and women and a few children had gathered on the other side of the Rio Grande. Twenty feet of shallow water separated two cultures.

The sheriff was about to speak when he heard a horse's hooves pounding hard toward them. The people moved out of the way as Godfrey Hamilton raced up to the edge of the water.

He heard part of the last speech of the chief's, about the white men not coming across the river.

"Damnation!" Hamilton thundered. He had studied to be a Baptist preacher and had learned how to use his good voice. "I won't have some heathen savage tell me what I can and can't do. I bought that property a year ago. Now I'm starting to build my ranch house out here and begin my horse-breeding ranch. Ain't no damn Pueblo Indian gonna tell me what to do as the mayor of Taos—"

Sheriff Murdock held up his hand and faced the whites and Mexicans. "Hold on now, there, Mr. Hamilton. How'd you like it if somebody started digging up and leveling off the Taos graveyard, knocking down your kin's headstones, covering them up with dirt? The old Indian has a point here. Let's see if we can work this out peaceable."

"Damnation peaceable!" Hamilton shouted. He spurred his white stallion forward, into the stream, spraying and splashing water as he charged across to the far side. There he rode straight at the burial platform and would have crashed into it, but half a dozen warriors ran out holding their eight-foot lances pointing forward.

At the last second, Hamilton jerked his stallion to the left to avoid the metal lance points and crashed directly into a young Indian man, who took the plunging horse's knees in his chest and went down. The stallion pranced, trying to get away from the thing under its feet. A dozen frantic steps by the heavy horse's hooves smashed into the writhing body, cut and tore at the soft form of the Pueblo warrior, before the stallion broke free.

Hamilton took one look at the ravaged, bleeding Indian on the ground. He bellowed in disbelief, turned his horse, and raced downstream and away from the terrified and angry Indians.

Several warriors raised rifles and bows as the horse began its run away from the dead Indian. A sharp word from Chief Running Fox stopped any firing.

The whites and Mexicans on the far shore were shocked by this sudden turn. Most of them slipped away quietly. Some of the men laughed and said that was one less damn Indian to worry about.

Longarm and the sheriff stood and watched the old Indian chief. He shook his head. Jennifer still stood beside the chief, watching him.

He spoke quietly to Jennifer, and she nodded, waded through the water, and went to the sheriff.

"Sheriff Murdock. My grandfather, Chief Running Fox, says the man who killed Red Feather must be turned over to the tribe so he can face Pueblo justice. He says last year when a warrior killed a white man in a fight, he had to face the white man's laws. This is the same. We will give you three days to find this man on the white horse and turn him over to our tribe."

Sheriff Murdock looked at Longarm. "Judas in a bucket, Longarm. What the hell we gonna do now?"

"First thing you better do is get the rest of these people back into town and let things simmer down a little. Maybe some kind of a compromise can be worked out."

The old sheriff nodded and started calling for those left near the river to clear the area, to get back into town before anybody else got into trouble out here.

The people left reluctantly.

The sheriff and Longarm stood with Jennifer watching the warriors work repairing the mounds that the two white men had started to level. Soon the mounds were rebuilt, and the Indians posted a guard around the area. All had rifles.

Jennifer waded across the stream and talked with her grandfather again. When she came back, she walked toward town with Longarm and Sheriff Murdock.

"I suggest you have a talk with this man on the white horse," Longarm said. "He's in trouble. Find out what he'll agree to do or to pay in place of getting fried over a small camp fire head-down."

The sheriff grunted. "First the Johnson murder, now Godfrey Hamilton, the mayor and richest man in town, kills a Pueblo. Things getting complicated around here. Never are easy, I guess." The old lawman looked up. "Longarm, you have any suspects for me on this Johnson slicing?"

"Not yet, but I'm working on it. Hamilton sounds like a bigger problem for you. If he doesn't do something, you could have a full-scale revolt on your hands. Remember what these same Pueblo Indians did to the Spanish back in 1680? They

17

killed over two thousand Spaniards and drove the priests and the rest of the Spanish out of the whole territory."

"Don't remind me," Sheriff Murdock said and turned down the street toward his office.

Jennifer Walking Dove touched Longarm's shoulder. "What are we going to do?"

"Not much we can do about the man on the white horse. The sheriff will talk to him. You can talk to your grandfather, see if he will compromise somehow. You might have some ideas that he would accept."

She nodded, her dark eyes serious, her short black hair bouncing. "Yes, I will talk to him. We must have a compromise. There must be no war between our people."

"While that's going on, I want to see the second puzzle that Wallace left for you. You said this one is harder?"

"It certainly is. I can't make any sense out of it at all."

She hesitated.

"Show me the puzzle, and then you can go and talk with your grandfather. No real damage to the graves. The mounds are only markers, aren't they?

She nodded. "That and more. Yes, come to my house and I'll show you the puzzle, then I must have a long talk with my grandfather."

An hour later, Longarm still puzzled over the items that lay on the kitchen table: a picture of a rattlesnake, uncoiled, head up; a picture of Taos's main street; a picture of a small saw; a book; a picture of a young baby; and a picture of a church with a heavy X marked over it.

Longarm worried over just what in hell this strange collection of clues could mean. The rattlesnake could show that the man was dangerous, that he struck suddenly with deadly results. The picture of Taos must indicate that the embezzler was in town. The saw? How did that apply to anything? How could that tie in with the other items?

The last three were even less rewarding. A book, that might mean the man Longarm hunted could read, maybe even that he was a serious student of some profession. Which one?

The picture of the baby confounded Longarm. How could a baby have anything in common with a rattlesnake and a saw? The picture of a local church cut from the newspaper and with a heavy X across it threw him completely. It made no sense. Well, it could tie in with the rattlesnake. The man they sought was dangerous and didn't go to church. Not much of a start.

After another hour of Longarm's silent cursing at the six clues he was no further along. None could be grouped or teamed. They seemed to be nonsense.

Jennifer rattled the back door and came into the kitchen. She looked at the clues and then back at Longarm.

"Not much progress," he said.

"Me, too. They don't mean a thing to me. But if that's all we have to help us find Wallace's killer, I'll stare at them until I go blind."

She looked at them a minute more, then took the church picture and put it beside the rattlesnake. "About as far as I got," Longarm said.

Jennifer brightened. "Oh, my Grandfather, Chief Running Fox, wants to talk to you. How about right now? You can talk and I'll show you around the pueblo."

"Much better than staring at this table. Let me find my hat."

The pueblo buildings were less than a quarter of a mile upstream from the village of Taos. They could see the seven-storied adobe structures as soon as they passed some trees. The adobe walls of each story supported the walls above, and long poles formed the ceilings and floor of each level.

"Most families have three rooms in the pueblo," Jennifer told Longarm. "When more are needed, if the family grows, more rooms are built on."

As they came closer, Longarm saw that the adobe blocks had been plastered with more of the adobe clay to give a smooth outer surface. He looked curiously at the ladders that went up to the roofs of all the first-floor rooms.

"The entrances to these ground-floor areas are through the roof," Jennifer said. "In early days, when our people were attacked, they simply lifted up the ladders and left them on the roofs, and the attackers had no way to get inside the buildings."

They saw children running around and a few women in the plaza in front of the structures.

"Most of the men are in the fields working on their crops," Jennifer said. "The men grow the beans and squash and corn,

19

and the women harvest it and store it for later use."

Longarm stood at the bottom of the largest of the structures and stared upward. It was seven stories, with only a few rooms on the top. A series of ladders led from one level to the next, and the whole thing had the rough shape of a pyramid.

Jennifer caught his hand. "We go up this ladder. Grandfather has come down to the first level to talk to you. He is old and doesn't move as well as he once did. He is terribly concerned about the man who killed Red Feather."

They climbed the wooden ladder, the rungs of which were tied in place with rawhide. On the roof Longarm saw another ladder, which extended downward into the room. The roof met others, and he saw women and children working and playing on them. The roofs of the ground-floor structures were also the floors of the second-story buildings.

Jennifer went down the ladder into the room below, and Longarm followed.

It was small, about ten feet square, with poles extending from the walls in several places. On these pegs were hung baskets containing food, clothing, and other goods the household used.

Blankets had been rolled up and placed by the wall. Longarm figured the blankets were spread out for sleeping and then taken up during the day.

"We Pueblo people spend most of our time outside," Jennifer said. "The rooms are used mostly at night or when the weather is bad. Most of the families have three rooms. One is for storing food, firewood, clothing, and other family items.

"In one of the other rooms we sleep, and in the other one we have our fire and do our cooking."

"Cool in the summer and warm in the winter," Longarm said, looking at the thick adobe walls.

Chief Running Fox walked through the door. Behind him came a shy young woman wearing a manta, a one-piece garment that looped over the left shoulder and left the right shoulder and arm bare. She carried mugs of cold water and a platter with cakes made from corn. She put them down beside the chief and then left without a word.

Jennifer introduced Longarm to her grandfather, and they sat down on blankets on the floor.

"I have some English," Chief Running Fox said.

"Chief Running Fox, I thank you for stopping your young warriors from firing at the man on the white horse," Longarm said. "You prevented a fight that could have resulted in a war between our people. We don't want that."

"All the Pueblo people ask for is justice," the chief said. "It is Pueblo law that must be followed."

"Sometimes the law can be harsh and even unjust. We grieve for your young man, but it was an accident. Hamilton did not plan to kill the warrior, don't you agree?"

"He did not plan to, but he did."

"When the Pueblo warrior killed the white man last year, the court called it an accident. The warrior did not die; he only went to prison."

"That is white man's law, judged by white men. Now we judge this Hamilton by Pueblo law."

"Sometimes the Pueblo law can also be harsh, not the best for all concerned," Longarm said. "We suggest a solution that will help everyone instead of killing another man."

"Pueblo always follow Pueblo law." The old chief looked away, sipped the water, and turned to his granddaughter. They spoke for a minute or two in their native tongue. Jennifer looked at Longarm.

"My grandfather says you are a pleasant white eye, but you are still a white eye. He does not wish to talk about the matter any more. He reminds you that there are only two-and-a-half days to the deadline to turn in the killer."

Chief Running Fox stood with some hesitation. He smiled at Jennifer, looked sternly at Longarm, and walked out of the room.

"I tell my grandfather he is as stubborn as a white-eye mule. He says it is good to be stubborn—when you are right. He says he will talk no more of it unless the Taos town chief comes."

"The mayor?"

"The mayor in Taos is the president of the city council."

"Who's that?"

Jennifer frowned. "That's the problem. The council president is Godfrey Hamilton."

"Oh, damn. If Hamilton is tried by the Pueblo council, what will the sentence be?"

"Death. It is the only penalty for taking another life."

"Somehow we have to work this out."

"Somehow, yes." She watched him where he sat on the rug. "We have many things to work out. Let me show you the rest of the pueblo. Our people have lived in this area for more than two hundred years. Some think our ancestors have lived in this area more than eight hundred years. We were here before the pilgrims landed at Plymouth Rock. We were here before the Spanish came and tried to convert us all to Christianity.

"Now there are more Mexicans here than there are Pueblos, and there are more whites here than there are Pueblos. Sometimes we feel that everyone is taking our country away from us."

Jennifer lifted her brows. "That seems to be the pattern when a stronger people move into the land of a weaker people. Somehow the Pueblos must survive. Now the tour."

She took him back up the ladder then up other ladders until they were at the top of the seven-storied structure. He noticed that the walls of the rooms near the top were thinner than those below.

The first-floor walls were eighteen inches thick and made of sturdy adobe blocks baked in the hot sun until they were rock hard. "Will you build higher than seven stories?"

She shook her head. "I don't know. An engineer in Santa Fe told me one day that the pueblos could never be higher than three stories due to the great weight of the adobe. I didn't tell him he was wrong."

They worked their way down to the ground, and she caught his hand.

"Now, come and I'll show you the fields down by the river and the way the men irrigate the crops. We grow dry beans and corn and squash, and I have brought back onion seeds, and now we raise onions and peppers as well. I tried to get our people to raise potatoes, but they don't like them."

The narrow fields along the headwaters of the Rio Grande River had been worked up to the very limit of the irrigation process. Ditches had been dug as high as possible on the stream, and the water run down to the crops below.

Longarm saw waving fields of corn and climbing bean bushes and hundreds of fast-growing squash and pumpkin plants.

He noted the tools the Indian men used. They could have done a better job with a plow or two and some good spades and hoes.

22

As they walked back to the pueblo, Jennifer told him how she had met Wallace Johnson and how they were attracted to each other immediately.

"He was five years older than I was, but I knew at once he was right for me. He said it didn't matter to him if I was a Pueblo or a Russian or a Chinese, as long as I was me. I loved him." She blinked rapidly to fight off tears.

"Now, Custis Long, we must get back to my house and work on the puzzles so we can unmask this embezzler and killer."

They worked over the table for the rest of the afternoon. The rattlesnake and the church with the X through it were side by side. The others baffled them.

"A saw, so the man saws something," Longarm said. "He could be a rich carpenter, a builder. He could sell saws or make them."

"The book isn't clear to me," Jennifer said. "He can read, he studies, maybe a teacher, but I'm the only one here. Could he be a preacher . . . ? Not likely. We have only the start of a library."

They were baffled by the picture of the new baby. They couldn't figure out how it could possibly tie in with a rattlesnake.

It was soon dark outside and Longarm suggested they go out for supper. They kept talking about the six clues as they ate, but gained no more ground on the answer to the puzzle.

"Try this," Jennifer said. "We know he's a rich man, one who doesn't go to church, is something of a snake, lives in Taos, likes to read and has a new baby."

They both laughed. That description might fit twenty or thirty men in Taos.

After supper he walked her home and decided he better get a good night's sleep and they would attack the puzzle the next day.

"Don't forget we need to figure out what to do about Mr. Hamilton. I won't allow there to be a war between the town and the Pueblos."

"I'll think on it," Longarm said.

He walked back to the hotel and up to his room on the second floor, number 222. He was tired. All of that brain work on the puzzle had worn him out as much as a twenty-mile ride.

Longarm put the key into the lock and turned it, then pushed open the door.

He did as always—stood behind the wall to the side of the door as he pushed it inward. The door had swung half open when the thunderous sound of a shotgun blasted into the silence of the high-altitude village. Hot lead slugs slammed through the open door, one taking off a four-inch section of the doorjamb and all of them plowing into the hall's plastered wall like a runaway freight train. Plaster dust and smoke from the burned powder filled the hall.

Longarm had pulled his hand back, but he wasn't quite fast enough. One of the double-aught buck slugs cut a half-inch slice along the top of his left wrist.

The deputy U.S. marshal dropped to the floor to look under the smoke in the room, but all he saw was a shotgun tied to the room's straight-backed chair and the string that had pulled the trigger when he pushed open the door.

"Missed me," Longarm said softly, then jolted into the room, pulling his cross-draw .44-40 six-gun with his right hand, hoping someone lurked inside.

Chapter 3

Longarm dove into the room where the shotgun had just fired, landed on his shoulder, and rolled coming to his feet. He couldn't see anyone in the place. A little light filtered in from the hall lamp and a bit of moonlight from the open window. The wind whipped the gunsmoke out of the room and the plaster dust from the hall.

After another quick check, Longarm knew there was no one in the room. Whoever had fixed the string on the trigger of the shotgun had made sure he wouldn't be caught in his own trap and exited out the window.

Longarm lit a lamp that sat on the dresser and surveyed the damage. His room had been thoroughly ransacked, his gladstone opened and clothing and spare ammunition dumped and scattered on the bed. The covers had been torn off it and the mattress moved as if someone had hunted for something under it.

By the time Longarm found the small pack of bandages and covered the gouge on his left hand, Sheriff Nathan Murdock had come in the door. The deputy U.S. marshal had not moved the shotgun, the chair, or even the string, which still stretched from the inside door handle upward to a screw in the door frame, then back and down to the shotgun trigger.

Sheriff Murdock looked at the shotgun and scowled.

"Who in hell did a setup like that? Ain't seen one of them in damn near twenty years."

"Glad I can still see it. Who in town knows about this sort of thing, Sheriff?"

"Twenty or thirty gents of questionable reputations I'd say offhand. More important, why was it set up in your room?"

"I like the way you think, Sheriff. We can narrow that twenty down to one. I'm here hunting one man, but I don't know who he is. Could be anybody, because I have no description."

The sheriff looked over the setup again. "You want to save this for sentimental reasons, or should we take it down afore it kills somebody?"

They removed the string and the screw. The knot on the door was a common shoestring tie and proved nothing.

Sheriff Murdock reached for the sawed-off shotgun, but Longarm had it first. "Evidence. I'll be holding it for the trial when we catch the bastard."

The sheriff snorted. "First off, Longarm, you got to figure out who the varmint is."

The room clerk from below checked in and saw that the room was in liveable condition.

"Would you rather move to another room, Mr. Longarm?" the clerk asked.

"No mister on it, just Longarm, and no, don't want to move. Just as soon make it easy for the rat to find me again. Only this time I'll be the one doing the shooting."

The clerk nodded and left to complete the cleanup in the hall with his bucket of water, dustpan, two towels, and a box filled with dust and plaster from where the double-aught had made its presence known.

Sheriff Murdock stared at Longarm for a while. "Deputy Long, you take care of yourself. Got enough going on in town without having to tell Billy Vail one of his best men got himself shot full of holes in my jurisdiction."

"You know Billy?"

"Only by official letters and telegrams." The older man groaned as he headed for the door. "Damn rheumatiz. I best be getting home for a spell. Don't figure on coming out again till morning, so you behave yourself."

Longarm grinned at the old lawman and shut the door after him. That was when he realized that the length and pull of the line had been judged so that the door had to be fully open, exposing the body of the person coming inside, before it set off the shotgun's trigger. That way the full effect of the thirteen to fifteen double-aught .32-caliber balls would be felt by the human body opening the door. He was damned lucky he'd taken the precaution of standing beside his door when he pushed it open. Whoever set up this little death trap had known what he was doing.

Longarm gathered up his clothes and goods and packed most of them back in his gladstone. He found that his spare Colt Model T 44-40 was still in place, wrapped in a pair of trousers.

Longarm pushed the back of the wooden chair under the doorknob so that anyone coming in would have to smash the chair to get through the door.

He dropped on the bed fully clothed and took out one of his three-for-a-nickel cheroots. Longarm took his time wetting the wrapping leaf of tobacco, then cut the end off the stogie and lit it with a wooden kitchen match.

He snapped the match into flame with his thumbnail, the way he always did. Only once, years ago, had the burning part of the matchstick broken off and lodged under his thumbnail. It burned like fury for several seconds.

That had cured him of lighting matches with his thumbnail for a while, but gradually the old habit came back. It was so much simpler.

Now, who had tried to blow him into hell?

He had been in town less than twelve hours, and already somebody had a gun out for him. There could be only one answer to the who question. The man was the embezzler, the same man who had killed Wallace Johnson.

The problem was finding out who it was, then capturing him and taking him back to Denver for trial.

He puffed on the cheroot and thought, but he could see nothing but the second set of clues the dead man had left for his lady friend, to help solve the puzzle.

The knock on his door was tentative, cautious. Longarm came to his feet off the bed in a splash of a second, his boots not making any noise. He strode to the wall next to the door knob.

"Who is it?"

"A friend, please let me in."

He frowned. It was a she-male. Why?

Without a sound he lifted the chair away from the door and twisted the key in the lock. When he opened the door, it was with a wide swing, and his Colt .44–40 covered whoever might be standing there.

To his surprise she was tall, with soft brown hair and a slender body that fascinated more than stirred him.

"Mr. Longarm?"

He nodded. "Who are you?"

"May I come in, I have a message for you."

Longarm figured he'd probably regret it, but he stepped back and allowed the tall creature to walk into his spider's web. She had no reticule, and there wasn't enough dress to hide anything. He doubted if she had a derringer between her legs.

He closed the door behind her and leaned against it.

"Who are you?"

"My name is Natasha, but that's not important. I've come to give you a message from a man you need to know better. My friend is a most important man in Taos. He wishes you well, but he also has a warning for you. Someone here may try to harm you."

She looked up at him, and he realized again how tall she was. At least five-feet-eight, tall for a woman when the average was about five-three. She had a pleasant face, but her soft brown hair worn long around her shoulders was her best feature. It glistened and shone, and was thick and heavy, yet it bounced with her every movement.

Natasha's face was an oval, with deeply placed eyes set wide apart over a small nose and a cupid mouth. Her eyes were checking Longarm out as he watched her.

"Someone tried to kill me tonight. If they'd succeeded, you'd have been too late, Natasha."

"I'm glad they missed you. I find you most . . . stimulating. May I show you something?"

"I never say no to a pretty lady."

She turned her back to him, and when she faced him again, the tight dress she wore was open to the waist, showing small naked breasts and a slender torso. She walked toward him slowly, caught his hands, and moved them over her breasts, then down between her legs.

"Just so you know that I carry no weapons and am not the one who is trying to harm you. Do you like Natasha?"

"Beautiful, Natasha, and . . . different. I like tall ladies. Shall I lock the door?"

"Yes, please, and put the chair back where you had it under the knob. I heard you move it."

"You also heard me come to the door?"

"Yes, and the bed squeak as you came off it, and three steps to the side of the door in case I had a shotgun. You are good. Some say I am also good at this kind of work."

She smiled at him as she said it, ducked under his arm, and in one swift, much practiced move, jerked his cross-draw Colt from his leather and pointed it at the ceiling.

"Poof, and you could have been dead."

Longarm grinned. Yes, she had fooled him, but he wouldn't let her know it.

"I let you do that so you'd feel good," he lied.

Natasha reached up and pulled down his face with one hand and kissed him. As she did, she slid the Colt back in his leather. The kiss was strange—not hard; her tongue did not touch him, but it felt as if his whole mouth were on fire. She nibbled at his lips, then kissed his eyes and took a quick step away from him. He hadn't had time to put his arms around her.

"So, Mr. Custis Long, you will be more careful, no?"

"Yes, Miss Natasha, I will be much more careful. I should check again. You may have hidden something, even a razor blade."

She smiled. "Now you are learning. Women make the best assassins, did you know that? In Europe the best assassins for hire are female. We are less suspect; we can move softly and quietly; and we can gain entrance for sexual purposes where no man could get in."

"How many men have you killed, Natasha?"

She smiled, and he could see her soft brown eyes turn harder. "For the professional there is no need to count. But I know you are a federal lawman, so I will hurry to tell you I have killed no one in this great country."

Custis Long was fascinated. A woman killer. The sight of her pert, small breasts hadn't stirred him at first, but now he felt the reaction. The kiss had been the capper, and now his short arm was longer than his name.

29

"I really must insist on a complete search, Natasha, now that you have raised the issue of risk. I'm afraid I'll have to take off all of your clothes."

"What an interesting idea. What if I refuse?"

"You won't." He bent and kissed her hard on the lips. This time her mouth was open and her tongue challenging him. He caught her and lifted her, and carried her the few feet to the bed. There he let her down gently, never breaking the kiss.

She stretched out and he lay directly on top of her, his erection pushing hard into her crotch. She made a small noise in her throat, then her eyes closed and her arms came around him, and Longarm wondered for just an instant who was seducing whom.

She helped him with the dress. She got up to remove it and stood there in her whalebone corset that was not really needed, pantaloons, a garter belt, and silk stockings that vanished into high-button shoes.

"Cuter than a bucket full of month-old puppies," Longarm said. "You ladies sure know how to dress to get a man's pecker up. Damn but them garter belts was invented by the devil himself, or maybe some sex-starved she-devil."

Natasha sat down and began undressing him.

"Oh, Natasha, did this friend of yours who told you to deliver the message say that you should spend the night with me?"

"What a terrible thing to ask, Deputy U.S. Marshal Custis Longarm Long. What a naughty thing to say." She bent over and kissed his lips, that light, lightning-rod kind of kiss that made him shiver. She smiled. "Staying all night is my idea. For a handsome man, Mr. Long, you do carry on. Are you all talk and no action?"

An hour later they sat on the edge of the bed, and Natasha admitted that they had experienced at least a little action. The poking had been better than Longarm had expected, and after two times they decided to rest a bit.

"Have you ever killed a man while making love to him?" Longarm asked.

Her eyebrows went up. "What a perfectly awful thing to ask, Mr. Long. Of course I have, that's when a woman has the advantage over a larger, stronger man. Especially if all she has is a knife in her corset." She laughed as he reacted.

"That's right, Longarm. You didn't inspect my corset well, did you? There is a knife there. I keep it but only for emergencies, now that I've left the business."

Longarm moved over a little so he could see her better. He nodded. "I thank my grandfathers for that small development."

She laughed. "I was working for my country, for the good of Mother Russia. It was an exciting time."

"At least you lived through it." He watched her. "You never did tell me who your friend is who was so kind as to send a warning to me about my safety."

"Oh, I thought you knew. Godfrey Hamilton, the richest man in town. Also the one the Pueblo Indians want to roast over a slow fire for killing that poor Indian man."

"Hamilton has enough to worry about himself without being concerned about me. He give you any reason for his warning?"

"Yes. He knows you're a deputy U.S. marshal and anything the Indians do is your concern, legally. He said he thinks you can help settle them down so they won't insist on toasting him or going to war. Either one would be bad for his businesses here in town."

"A logical, reasonable man. Thank him for me, for his warning and for his messenger."

Her hand curled around his limp penis. Slowly she worked on him until it started to rise.

"I'll give him your thanks, and my own, but not tonight." She kept working on his slowly building erection. "What's the one thing you wish a woman could do for you?" She had him fully erect now and bent down so her breasts rubbed up and back against his sensitive shaft and head.

"Wish a woman would do?"

"You must have some fantasy. What's the wildest?"

"Well, a woman has her three holes."

Natasha yelped in delight. "And we've only used one of mine. Now I want to show you how sweet it can be in one of the other ones. I want to suck you off until you explode down my throat. Does that sound exciting?"

She bent then and kissed his erection. She washed him down with her tongue, wetting him all over, then did the same to his balls. Longarm squirmed on the bed.

"Jeeze but that feels just ever so fine," he said.

"Just getting started."

Slowly she drew him into her mouth, nibbling at his shaft as she inched it in. He nearly came the first minute, then settled down to make it last.

She was a master at her work. Natasha nibbled and sucked and then slowly began to pump up and down on him, her head bobbing in a slow rhythm that started his motor running almost at once. Her teeth barely scraped against his sensitive head as she came almost off him, then slowly inched him back into her until her lips touched his shock of pubic hair.

Natasha worked slowly, gradually building up the pace, constantly adding little nips and swirls and dartings with her tongue as she pumped and sucked and kept him moving on the bed, not wanting to do anything to speed a climax but unable to lie still.

"Damn, woman, finish me off and put me out of my misery!" Longarm pleaded, grunting and writhing under her.

She speeded up the movements, then came almost off him again, and he screeched at the near loss of her. She resumed her head movements at an increased pace.

Longarm lay there gritting his teeth, trying to hold back to make the intense, exquisite pain and glory of it last longer. His hips thrust forward without any help from him. She let out a muffled sound, then pulled back a little, so she wouldn't strangle, and accepted his movements.

Longarm swore softly under his breath. His hips pumped up in this unnatural position, stroke after stroke. They came faster and faster, until he couldn't put it off any longer and the overwhelming gushing of emotions ripped through him. He felt his hips jerk in an automatic spasm, then again and again until he had spewed his molten life substance into her.

Natasha swallowed again and then again, keeping pace with him and coming away from him only when he at last settled down and sighed and his stiffness began to go limp.

She turned and kissed him, and he held her closely to his chest.

She murmured something, and he made sure she kept her hands on the bed. In this state he wouldn't be hard to knife to death, and she had told him how good she was at it.

He chuckled. She was out of the business. She had been in

the business of assassination for her government? He shook his head. He must have heard wrong.

Sometime later, he wasn't sure just how late it was, he awoke and looked at her. Oh, damn, what a session. Three times, or four, or five, he couldn't remember. The moon, which he had seen out the window earlier, had scuttered far out of sight. She lay against him heavily now, perhaps sleeping.

He moved, and she stirred, then lifted away from him and sat up. "Darling man, you could have been dead by now. I'm glad I'm out of the business."

Before she could say another word, Longarm's .44-40 eased against the side of her head, and he cocked the hammer back with a deadly click.

"Not too dead, I'd say, Natasha. Not me at least. I always like to keep my ass covered."

She turned. "Just maybe I've met my match. It would be interesting to have a contest. But if we do, one of us would die. Do you want that?"

"No, Natasha. I have no reason to see you die. What good would it do? Perhaps we can work together sometime, on some especially devilish villain who needs to be brought down, and the law can't touch him."

Natasha smiled. "I like that. Now it's sleep time. Tomorrow you must find the killer who murdered that young man in his buggy."

"How do you know that?"

"Everybody in town knows. You come to see him, now must find his killer. Everyone knows, especially the man you look for, the embezzler, right?"

Chapter 4

Just at daylight the next morning, Natasha stirred in the bed beside Longarm, and he lifted the Colt in an automatic reflex.

She kissed his cheek.

"Relax, good lover, I won't hurt you. I must hurry back to my room in the big house with my patron, Mr. Hamilton. I will give him your thanks."

Longarm put down the Colt and watched her dress. She was thin, so her breasts seemed larger and her hips flared just enough to make her woman. He was amazed at what a good lover she was. Technique, not equipment, was the key to any good lovemaking, he realized, again.

She dressed quickly, leaving off the silk stockings, brushed a quick kiss across his cheek, and rushed out the door. He sat on the bed, shook his head to clear it, and then got up. Five-thirty, be full light soon.

After shaving closely in the cold water from the old-fashioned pitcher and bowl, he dressed in his town clothes—beige pants, tan shirt, black leather vest, and his snuff-brown Stetson with the flat crown—and headed out for breakfast. He didn't want hotel food this morning.

Longarm settled for a café halfway down the street, on the other side. It looked to be filled with locals, and so he figured it must be good. He had a six-high stack of hotcakes, two eggs, three mugs of Arbuckle, and a dozen strips of bacon.

A young man came up to his table, hat in hand. Longarm looked up.

"You all find him yet?"

"What was that?"

"You all find that guy what killed the kid in the buggy?"

"No, I'm afraid not. Did you slice his throat open?"

The young man chuckled and shook his head. "Reckon not, Mr. Marshal. I don't like knives. I'd a shot him."

"Looks like you're in the clear then. You figure out who killed him, you let me know, and I'll deputize you."

"Yes, sir," the kid said and walked away with a slight swagger to his cowboy bowed legs.

Longarm headed for the schoolmarm's house. It was still early, but he figured she'd be up and decent.

Jennifer Walking Dove, the schoolmistress, answered the door on the first knock. It was as if she'd seen him coming and waited by the panel.

"Good morning!" she said with a lilt to the words that immediately made Longarm feel better. She brushed at the short black bangs across her forehead and smiled. It was a smile to remember.

"I figured out something else about the clues in the second puzzle," she said. Then she frowned. "I'm sorry, my manners. Mr. Long, please come in. Have you had any breakfast?"

"Just et, Miss Jennifer. I thank you."

She closed the door and led him to the small dining room table where they had left the puzzle pieces.

"Before we decided that the rattlesnake and the church with the X through it went together. The killer is a man who strikes suddenly with deadly force and who is not a churchgoer. I got to looking at the picture of the Taos main street."

"We figured he was from town here," Longarm said.

"Yes, but look at the stores we can identify. Two of them are owned by Godfrey Hamilton."

"How long has Hamilton been in town?"

She furrowed her brow, and Longarm liked the way it set off her pretty face.

"I'd say I can remember him when I was . . ." She stopped. "Oh, I can remember him back at least twelve or fifteen years."

"Then it couldn't have been him. Our killer had to have been in Denver at that time. We know our man is from town; that's probably all we can get out of that picture."

He put the picture up by the snake and the church. "Now that leaves us with the picture of a saw, a book, and a picture of a newborn baby. What can the saw mean? A carpenter, an architect, a construction contractor?"

"There are other uses for saws. He could even be a butcher who uses a meat saw."

Longarm nodded. "Good thinking. We've got to expand our ideas about the picture. I'm trying to think what I'd do if I had fifty thousand dollars in cash. Let's say I wound up here in Taos. A man has to do something, can't just sit around all day and stare at beautiful women and make dreams.

"Would I own a store, or a saloon? Maybe a gambling hall and the thrill of the cards? Or would I be a lawyer, maybe, or own a big ranch? What would the man do who stole all that money?"

"With that much money he'd want to be somebody," Jennifer said. "I mean he'd want to own something or be boss or learn something new, or you know, be somebody."

"Who is *somebody* here in town? The sheriff, Godfrey Hamilton, a preacher or two, the city councilmen, a banker, maybe a big gambling hall owner. Did any of the important men come to town recently and maybe seem to be hiding his past?"

Jennifer shook her head, and her short black hair bounced from side to side. Her pretty face was fixed in a worried look. "I think and I think, but none of those men seem to fit the pattern, and remember from puzzle number one, he has to be rich or at least have quite a bit of money."

They both stared at the pictures.

"The book must mean there is some learning involved," Longarm continued. "That could be a preacher, a lawyer, a teacher, something like that. I guess the college professor is out. What about lawyers?"

Jennifer talked about the two lawyers in town. One had been there for some years, she couldn't remember how many. The other one was not more than twenty-five so he couldn't be a suspect.

"The baby picture bothers me," Longarm said. "How can it fit in with these other clues?"

36

"Maybe it isn't the baby itself," Jennifer said. "It could be what the baby does, or eats or wears."

"That one I'm going to have to come back to. We've just about eliminated the richest man in town, Hamilton. He's been here too long. I'm going to see if I can trace Wallace's movements that last day. Want to come along? With your help I'll get more information."

She nodded, put on a small hat and a light jacket over her dress, and they walked downtown. Wallace had lived at the hotel, so they began there. His room hadn't been released yet by the sheriff and was still the way Wallace had left it.

Jennifer teared up as they looked through the room and through the things he had owned. Behind the bed and crumpled up, Longarm found a piece of yellow paper. They spread it out and smoothed it, and Jennifer read the penciled words.

"Johnson: Meet me at the bridge near Devil's Canyon just after midnight and we'll agree to some kind of restitution."

"Where's Devil's Canyon?" Longarm asked.

"Not far from where they found the . . . the buggy."

"We'll see who in town sells paper like this. It's from some kind of a notepad. Let's keep looking."

In a dresser drawer under some clothes, they found a loaded derringer, a hefty .45-caliber type with two barrels and a box of spare shells.

"Wallace told me he never carried a gun. He said he wasn't much good with one and they scared him."

"He forgot to take this one with him that last night, or he might still be alive," Longarm said.

They searched the rest of the room thoroughly. Longarm stood at the door and scanned the place again. Would Wallace hide anything in his room? Was he the careful type of man who would make sure that what he knew wouldn't be lost?

On a chance, Longarm went back in the room, took out the dresser drawers, and looked at the bottom of each one. Jennifer watched him curiously. On the bottom of the last drawer he found a piece of yellow paper fastened with glue. He gently removed and unfolded it.

It was a kind of diary, with each date followed by what Wallace had experienced that day. Longarm and Jennifer scanned the sheet word by word.

"June 4: Arrived in Taos. Room at hotel. Asking questions.

"June 11: Checking suspects. I have ten or twelve. Men with money and position.

"June 12: Met Jennifer. What a sweetheart. I can't tell her what I'm doing.

"July 7: Letter arrived from Mother giving me description of man who swindled my father. Jennifer is a big help. I'm falling in love with her.

"July 10: Suspects down to three. Working on them every day. Jennifer knows the town so well. Going to take her back home with me.

"July 12: Almost sure who my father's killer is. Fits the description. Came to town short enough time ago. Working on it.

"July 13: Confronting the killer today. He's tall and thin, rich, and is trying to make up for what he did to my father. He'll never be able to do it.

"July 14: Second meeting set. He admitted nothing. I showed him evidence and he scoffed at it. Agreed to meet me tonight near Devil's Canyon for a long talk. Note came this afternoon confirming our meeting tonight. He'll never agree to go back to Denver, but maybe we can get compensation. I'll want the whole $50,000!"

That was the last entry in the log. Longarm stared at the yellow lined paper.

"Let's try and find out where they sell this kind of paper. Then we'll show this to the sheriff. He should know about it."

They checked the five stores in town that sold pads of paper. None of them had yellow lined pads in stock. Longarm and Jennifer took the note and the log to the sheriff.

"Don't help much, does it?" the old lawman said. He had one boot off and was rubbing his foot. "I got the foot aches, today. You know when you hit sixty and four, you get up every day and find a new place on your body that can hurt."

"Tall and thin, at least we have one clue to his description now," Longarm said.

"I'll keep a lookout for him," Sheriff Johnson said. "You talked that old chief, Running Fox, into some sense yet about us not having a war?"

"Working on it, Sheriff. He's a tough old bird. He's Jennifer's grandfather."

"Then, little Jennifer, you should be able to get him to stop the war. An Indian war won't do a damn bit of good. Just get a bunch more Indians and some whites killed."

They said good-bye and walked the dusty street again.

"July 14. Jennifer, any idea what you were doing that day? Did you meet Wallace for lunch or dinner or anything?"

"No. He said he had a lot of loose ends to get tied up on the case he was on and that he'd see me the next day for breakfast at my house. He never came."

"Did he gamble, drink, play pool? Where would he hang out until it was time for that midnight meeting?"

"He said he spent some time at the Alonzo Pool Hall, down the street here a ways. It's not a place I'd want to go."

Longarm nodded. "Figures, but you can stay outside while I ask some questions."

The man who ran the pool hall and served drinks on the side was Alonzo himself. Longarm never did get a last name.

"Wally? Yeah, he spent some time here. Damn good with a cue. Said he had lots of practice. Shame about him going over the side. Hear somebody knifed him first, that right?"

"It is. I'm wondering if he made any enemies in here, you know, a small bet on a pool game?"

"No, sir, Marshal, no gambling in here. No, sir."

Longarm grinned. "Don't worry, I don't have any jurisdiction here in town on that score. I'm just hunting my man."

"Well, he did do some small wagers. You know, maybe a dollar a game. Nothing to get killed over. He did win most of the time."

"You have a pad of paper around? I need to write myself a note."

Alonzo brought out a pad about the size of his hand. The paper was white and glued at the top. Longarm wrote a couple of words, tore off the page, and pocketed it. It was nothing like the yellow pad he was looking for.

"Thanks. Any idea if he did any serious drinking at a saloon or gambling hall?"

"He did mention the Palace Saloon. Said they had women there who would show you their tits to get you upstairs. I been in there twice and I never seen any tits."

"Maybe they knew you wouldn't buy, Alonzo. Thanks, I'll go over and see if I can see any of those pretty orbs."

Outside, Longarm told Jennifer Walking Dove what he had learned.

"He probably played most of his pool before he met you," he said.

They walked down to the saloon, and Jennifer told him she'd be in the dress shop next door. Longarm strolled into the saloon, ordered a needled beer, and looked around. Two girls came up to him at the bar. They flipped a silver dollar. The winner took the silver dollar and Longarm, and the other one left.

"You busy, big man? Looks like you're the kind of gent who would buy a girl a whiskey."

"Only if it's rye and I get to taste it first," Longarm said.

The woman laughed. "You've been here before. I'm Lotta, you wanta have a lotta fun? I'm your girl. Hey, biggest tits in the place. For a quarter I'll give you a look."

"Lotta, I don't pay to look at a naked woman. But those sure are good tits. I might have a spare silver dollar for the right information."

"Hey, for that you get to feel my tits." She popped open her blouse and showed him. They were big, with red nipples that had been rouged and areolas that had been brightened with cosmetics as well.

"You like Lotta's big boobs? All yours upstairs for a skinny three dollars."

"I'd rather spend this cartwheel. Lotta, you ever talk to the kid who got himself murdered here a couple of nights ago?"

"You mean Wally Johnson. Sure I know him. Flashed my tits at him a couple of times for free, but he wouldn't screw."

"You ever see him talk to anybody in here, maybe get into an argument or a fight?"

"Wally? Hell no. He was a gentleman, soft-spoken, kindly. Said I had the best tits in town but he wasn't buying. He usually sat in on the nickel poker games, sometimes played solitaire by himself. Not much of a mixer. Never did go upstairs. Hey, I'm sorry somebody slit his throat. Hope you catch the son of a bitch."

"I hope so, too, Lotta. You take care of them tits and don't let them catch cold."

"Hey, what about my silver dollar?" She flashed her breasts at him again, and he chuckled and flipped her the silver wheel. Longarm finished his needled beer and walked outside.

Jennifer waited for him just beyond the dress shop.

"Nothing," he said. Jennifer didn't need to know about Lotta.

"Wallace ate most of his meals at the hotel. He said it was more convenient that way. We could ask there."

At the hotel they talked to the head waiter.

"Yes, I remember Mr. Johnson. A good tipper. He had been to Chicago he said and knew about tipping. But I never saw him dine with anyone except Miss Walking Dove. He was quiet, courteous, kind to the waiters, and always polite."

They thanked him and moved out to the street.

"I don't know why I thought that might help," Longarm said. "Figured that there might have been some kind of a public meeting between the two."

Jennifer let out a little cry of alarm. "Your hand, it's bleeding."

"Just a graze last night from the shotgun."

Her eyes flared with fear and her face went white. "Shotgun? What about a shotgun?"

He told her about it. She caught his right hand and turned him around. "We're going to see Doc Smith right now. It could get infected, and you could get blood poisoning and lose your hand."

"It's just a scratch."

"That's what a man in Santa Fe said my last year there. It was just a blister on his foot, and a month later he was dead. You come along now, and no arguments."

Her dark eyes flashed and she pulled him. Longarm chuckled but went along. Somehow it didn't seem so bad to have somebody worry about the state of his health for a change. They walked into the doctor's office and found no one waiting.

A woman came to a window and asked about the problem, then led them into a room and said Dr. Smith would be there soon. He came in a minute later, peeled off the quick bandage Longarm had used, and nodded.

"Gunshot?" he asked.

"Yeah, Doc. Just a graze. No problem. I didn't want to come in."

"No, better to be safe. Could get infected." He poured some smelly disinfectant over the wound, which made Longarm jerk his hand back in surprise and pain.

"More it hurts, more good it does," Dr. Smith said with a small gleam in his eye. He put some ointment over the half-inch-long groove and wrapped it with a white bandage.

"That should hold you for a while. See me in a week and we'll check how it's doing."

Longarm gave him two dollars, and he and Jennifer Walking Dove strolled down the street.

"Any more ideas about those clues?" he asked the young Indian girl.

"No, the baby picture is the one that stops me. How can it have any relation to the others?"

"It does. We just have to figure it out."

They had walked back near the bank when Longarm looked up, then turned to the north.

"We've got trouble."

"What was that sound?"

"Shots, rifle shots coming from up by the river and those Indian burial mounds."

"We better get up there," Jennifer said, and they turned and hurried toward the mounds. She ran almost as fast as he did even though she wore an ankle-length skirt.

They came around the last building and saw half a dozen Indian men hidden behind the mounds and some of the trees. Two more shots came from somewhere high behind them, near the building they had just passed.

Two shots answered from the mounds.

"Damned idiots!" Longarm huffed. He turned and ran to the back of the two-story wooden structure, which looked like a try to build a big warehouse. At the rear he found what he'd hoped he would. A wooden ladder had been nailed to the outside wall and extended all the way to the roof. He took the rungs two at a time as he climbed to the slanted roof.

He stepped over the low berm and fisted his Colt .44–40. Two men lay on the rooftop with rifles. One popped up and fired over the roof peak, then dropped down behind it. A rifle slug from the mounds answered him, thunking into the shingled roof on the other side.

Longarm put a .44–40 slug into the roof beside the man who had just fired.

"What the hell?" the man shouted, looking over his shoulder.

"Drop the rifles and crawl back here while you're still not full of lead," Longarm barked. "You two trying to start an Indian war all on your own?"

The two men crawled down from the roof peak and scrambled down the slope, eyes downcast.

"Hell, we was just having a little fun with the Injuns," one man said.

"You were?" Longarm asked. "That's like me saying I'm just having a little fun when I throw both of you off the top of this building to see how high you'll bounce."

"You ain't gonna do that are you, Marshal?"

"Damn well should. Toss them rifles to the ground. If you got any more firepower, toss it over the side, too."

"Could damage a good shooting iron if'n it hit a rock down there," the taller of the two said.

Longarm nodded. "I kinda hope it does. By the time you get down the ladder, the sheriff should be here. He'll have some nice friendly suggestions for you. I'm charging you with a federal violation for the attempted murder of those three Indians out there. You should get at least five years in prison for your little stunt. Now toss them rifles, get down the ladder, find your weapon, and then sit beside it with your fingers laced on top of your head."

By the time Longarm dropped down the ladder to the ground, Sheriff Murdock had arrived, and Walking Dove told him what had happened. He put handcuffs on the two, confiscated their handguns, and looked over at Longarm.

"Federal charges?"

"Damn right. Endangerment of wards of the federal government, and attempted murder. Walking Dove, can you get me the names of three of those men who were out there behind the grave mounds?"

She turned and hurried toward the river.

Sheriff Nathan Murdock took off a sweat-stained hat and scratched his wispy gray hair. "Longarm, this ain't gonna help matters nohow. You know who you corralled here? This gonna make the old boy fit to start a war all by himself. You just arrested the son of his honor himself, Godfrey Hamilton."

Chapter 5

Longarm stared at the sheriff as a deputy hustled the two men away toward the jail.

"One of those two is the son of Godfrey Hamilton, Taos's mayor and the hombre on the white horse that stomped that Indian to death?"

"Sure as hell is, Marshal Long. Kid's the apple of his eye, so as to speak."

Longarm grinned. "Good. That gives us one more lever to use on Hamilton. If he doesn't cooperate with us on this Indian thing, I'll see that his kid gets five to ten for attempted murder of wards of the United States government, the Indians. You be sure to tell him that when he comes down to the jail to bail out his kid."

Sheriff Murdock nodded. "Yeah, it might be a help after all. Danged if it might." He turned and walked toward the jail and the two prisoners.

Jennifer Walking Dove came hurrying up from the river.

"I know who three of the Pueblo men were over there, the ones the white men were shooting at. They said they'll be glad to testify in white man's court against the shooters."

Longarm grinned. At least something was starting to go right.

"If I'm going to help settle this Indian problem, I need to know a lot more about the tribe here. Think you can give me a detailed tour of the Pueblo lands and irrigation system?"

Jennifer smiled. It crinkled the corners of her dark eyes, and when she nodded, her short black hair bounced delightfully.

"Yes, but we should start right now. Do you want to walk or ride? The fields are only a mile away."

They walked, and she told him about the Pueblo people.

"No one is sure how long my people have lived in this area. Some say some of the early ruins are over eight hundred years old. We have lived here for so long because of the farming we do with the waters from the great river.

"About two hundred years ago there were many Spanish priests and soldiers here. They came up from Mexico and controlled the land and our lives.

"Then in 1680 our people rose up and overthrew the bad rule of the Spanish, drove every Spaniard out of the New Mexico area, killed a great many, and once again my people could live their lives in peace.

"One of the benefits of that uprising was the four or five thousand horses that the Spanish had brought here and that now had no owners."

Longarm helped Jennifer around a steep part of the path; then they walked along the river, toward a valley below.

"My people caught these animals and brought them into herds and used a few of them. Here in Taos we were a trading center for a great many Indian nations. They came here once a year to trade their goods for our food.

"When they saw the horses, they were amazed and at once knew how important they could be to the roving bands that crossed the wide plains and deserts.

"Soon Taos became the center not only for trading food-stuffs but horses as well. The Pueblos raised large herds of horses for this trading time. We still have many horses and sell them to anyone who comes.

"Now most of the tribes breed their own horse herds, but we always have more if they need them. You might say that the Pueblos were the ones who really introduced the horse to the many Plains Indian tribes such as the Comanches, the Kiowa, the Cheyenne, and the Utes and Shoshoni."

Longarm grinned. "I've got a few friends in the U.S. Army who wish that the Plains Indians had never found out about horses. But it's a little late for us to be complaining now."

They walked on toward the fields. "Do the tribes still come here for trading?"

"Not much anymore. They have little that we want. The buffalo are almost gone, and at one time they brought in buffalo robes and various other products made from the giant beasts. Now we raise our crops and get along the best we can."

They came to a wide place where the stream, which was the headwater of the mighty Rio Grande, had dug out a considerable valley. The rich topsoil had been deposited over many years of flooding, and now most of the valley had been planted with crops by the industrious Pueblos.

There were growing rows of corn, a field that Longarm decided was wheat, and other patches of foodstuffs he couldn't make out from the distance.

Each field was irrigated by a small ditch that brought water from higher up on the Rio Grande down to this lower field.

"This is our livelihood, Longarm," Jennifer said. "At one time only the women worked in the fields, but now the men work alongside them. The crops are important. If they do not grow well or wild animals come and eat them, our tribe will not have much to live on through the long, cold winter months."

They walked through the fields, and now Longarm could identify dry beans, squash, and melons growing in the fertile soil. Men worked at flooding the small plots, then shutting off the water. They had few tools and used mostly wooden paddles four or five inches wide and sharpened at the end.

Longarm remembered the futile attempts by the government to try to train the Plains Indians in growing their own food. The men wouldn't even try it; the women were little concerned. In those areas most of them had little good soil and not much water. This was an ideal situation for farming, and the Pueblos had taken advantage of it for what must have been eight hundred years.

Now the invading whites and the Mexicans were threatening their very existence.

Corn seemed to be the staple. It was easy to cultivate and could be stored for long periods of time. They walked again, checking the growth of the vegetables.

"I try to bring new things for them to grow, but some just don't work. I brought potatoes, but nobody seemed to like the taste of the potatoes. I'll try again whenever I go to Santa Fe.

There I spend a lot of time in a store that has a seed catalog with all sorts of good things in it."

They turned and walked back toward the big, rambling apartment houses the people called the pueblos.

"Let's get back and take a better look at those clues," Longarm said. "This diversion has cleared my mind; now maybe I can figure out how the pictures connect and get a better idea who the killer is. There must be a quicker way to smoke this man out of his perfect hiding spot here in Taos, but I can't figure out what it is."

Halfway back to the pueblos, Jennifer turned in at a faint trail. "Let me show you something," she said. He followed her off the main trail to a small green wonderland.

"A spring comes out of the slopes here and waters this small area; then the water is used up," she said.

Jennifer sat down on a swatch of green grass and looked up.

"Resting time," she said.

Longarm chuckled as he sat beside her. "Walking Dove, you could outhike me three times over if you wanted to. You're really not that tired, are you?"

She moved closer to him and shook her head. Her lips found his, and the sudden tingle of her kiss was surprising. She eased back from him and smiled.

"Remember, Longarm. I said that I would do anything you wanted me to do because you are helping to find this terrible killer. I have not forgotten. I didn't want you to forget." She kissed him again and gently pushed him back to the grass until she lay half on top of him.

Her lips burned against his; her breasts pushed against his chest, and he could feel the heat of them. Custis Long put his arms around Jennifer Walking Dove and held her tightly. He was in no rush to let the kiss end.

When it did, she pushed up slightly. "Would this be a good time, Longarm? We won't be disturbed here. It's a secret place but also private. It's often used by lovers, and no one breaks in on anyone."

Her hand stroked up to his crotch, and she found a growing hardness there.

"Yes, now, Longarm. You have done so much for me. I want to do this small thing for you." She lifted her brows.

"Oh, if you are wondering or worrying that I am a virgin, I am not. I have made love before."

She sat up and began to unbutton her blouse. He came up beside her and had just reached to help her when a rifle shot blasted into the silence of the high country glen.

Longarm groaned and slammed backward. He reached up and pulled Jennifer down beside him.

"You're shot!" she whispered.

"Just my arm, not too bad. Somebody didn't mind disturbing us here."

"Not a Pueblo. Never do that. Never shoot at you." Her face showed worry at his pain. "Can you move without hurting?" He nodded, and they crawled to a rank of taller grass and shrubs to hide. They faded farther back into the heavier growth of piñon pines and the tall ponderosa.

When they were out of sight of the gunman, Jennifer looked at Longarm's wound.

"It's bad," she said. "I better wrap it up."

"Later. You stay here. I want to see if I can find the bushwhacker. Stay until it's safe. Then hurry back to your house. I'll see you later there."

With that, Longarm faded into the brush and trees, and Jennifer thought he must be an Indian himself the way he moved without making a sound.

Longarm hurried now, striking a path at an angle to the trail back to town, so he could cut the trail ahead of the gunman.

He ran with his Colt in his right fist, eyes alert, never breaking a stick or letting a pine branch swing backward. It took him five minutes to get to the trail. There was no way he could find any tracks. He settled down in some piñon pine and shrubs and waited. He was hidden from anyone on the trail. He tied a kerchief around his upper left arm. The bullet had bored a neat hole through the outer arm, halfway between his shoulder and his elbow. It had either missed or just scraped the arm bone.

Five minutes later, a white man came jogging up the trail. He held a rifle in his hands and kept looking behind him. Longarm waited until the man was fifteen feet from him on the trail; then he put a round into the ground in front of him.

The man froze in place and slowly turned to look in the direction the shot had come from. He saw the black hole of the .44-40 muzzle aimed at his chest.

"Are you a dead man or do you know how to talk?" Longarm barked.

"I talk real good. Who be you?"

"I'm the guy you tried to kill. Your weapon must fire a little high and to the left, considering you had me with a heart aim."

"Didn't shoot nobody," the man said. His lower lip quivered. He looked to be about thirty, medium height, wore a brown hat and a light green shirt and dark pants.

"I been deer hunting. Had this buck dead to rights and he jumped."

"Sure, drop the rifle, then the six-gun. Do it now!"

The man looked hard and steady at Longarm.

"Try it, pilgrim, and you're deader than a twice-shot hummingbird in a hail of buckshot. You want that?"

"Never said I was drawing." Slowly he let the weapons fall to the ground.

"Now, down on your face on the ground. Gonna play a little Indian game called shoot the kneecaps. I blast both your knees, then let you make a run for it. I kind of wonder how far you'll get."

"You're a U.S. marshal. You'd never shoot an unarmed man."

"Hey, how come you know who I am? And who says you were unarmed? You have a rifle and a six-gun, more weapons than I do. Which knee first?"

"You can't do this."

"Why not? You see the sheriff anywhere around?"

"No."

"You think I like getting shot from ambush, especially when that sweet little girl was about ready to let me deflower her right there on the grass?"

"Oh, God."

"Ten seconds. You got ten seconds to talk before you lose your right knee."

"Dammit, he said it'd be easy."

"The guy who hires a killer always says that. So, killer, who hired you?"

"Don't know his name. Tall, thin gent. Stopped me on the street. We talked in an alley. Nobody saw us. He gave me

50

twenty dollars. I ain't seen twenty dollars cash in over two years. Damn tough going for me."

"What was his name?"

"Don't know. I just rode into town. Saw him near the livery where I put my horse. Then he called to me from the alley. Hell, I had only twenty cents in my purse. Four beers for supper."

Longarm didn't like the answers he'd got, but he figured they were the truth. Most men can't lie worth shooting. This one either.

"What did he look like?"

"Tall and thin, wore a black hat, a coat and tie. A gent, I'd say. Had a funny smell about him. First I thought he was the undertaker drumming up business, but wasn't that."

"Smell, you say. What did it smell like?"

"Don't know. Smelled it once before, but can't remember where or what it was."

"You think on it while I shoot you in the kneecap."

"No! I'm telling you all I know."

"What kind of shoes? Town shoes, boots, moccasins, miner boots?"

"Town shoes, black with a little pattern on the toes."

"What did his hands look like?"

"Too damn dark in the alley."

"You took a twenty-dollar bill from him. Smooth hands, rough, dirty, greasy, mine-stained?"

"Oh, clean hands. Fingernails clean and trimmed. Remember that. Unusual."

Longarm swore softly. He had a little more on the tall, thin man, but not much: clean hands and a smell. He was at the bottom of a dry well.

"Get up. See how you'll like the county jail for a time. Not much but better than getting your knees shot off."

A half hour later, Longarm had stashed the prisoner in the jail, lodged a complaint with the sheriff, and told him to keep the man for a week and then release him. Federal charge: attempted murder of a federal law officer.

Longarm made a stop at Dr. Smith's office. The sawbones looked surprised.

"Thought you were coming back in a week."

"Well, got something more interesting."

The doctor took off the pad and the kerchief and snorted. "Well, somebody is getting closer. One of these days you'll be over at the undertaker's office instead of mine. Let me see what we have here. Take off your shirt."

When he got outside, Longarm found that it was late afternoon. Somehow he had missed dinner. He took the back street and walked out to Jennifer's schoolmarm's house. By that time it was dusk and he saw a lamp burning in the window. He knocked on the back door and she rushed into his arms.

"I was so afraid for you!" she cried. The hug was long and tight, and he liked it. He reached down and kissed the top of her head, and she looked up. "I'm glad you're alive and well. How's the arm?"

"Doc Smith said I'd live. Now, where are those damnable pictures?"

He spent a half hour trying to get some new insights into them. Then he smelled fried chicken in the kitchen and went in and watched Jennifer finish getting supper: fried chicken, mashed potatoes and gravy, boiled carrots, and applesauce and cookies for dessert.

He told her about the bushwhacker. "I've got two charges against him," Longarm said. "He not only shot me, he interrupted what was going to be an interesting afternoon."

Jennifer Walking Dove blushed, then grinned. "It was going to be interesting and wonderful for me, too. Let's just say it was postponed for a while."

Supper was fine. Longarm leaned back and finished his coffee, then touched her hand.

"You don't have to feed me," he said.

"I want to. It's no fun cooking for just one. I have people over just so I can cook. Anyway, I still owe you. Make you a deal. You get back to the pictures and I'll do the dishes."

Longarm agreed to the tough terms and looked at the six pictures again.

The rattlesnake and the church with the X through it and the picture of Main Street were clustered together. That left the other three: a book and pictures of a newborn baby and a small saw. How could they relate to one another?

An idea hit him. What if this clue had two lines? The first would indicate a man who lived in town, who didn't go to church and could strike as quick and deadly as a rattlesnake.

Then the second line would be built around the last three clues. Like what?

Longarm worked on six different combinations and wrote them down on a pad of paper, but nothing worked. At last he put down the most plausible one. Something was wrong, but some of it was right. He came up with this: The book meant the embezzler was a professional man, the saw that a saw was involved in his work, and the baby that he liked babies. Longarm stretched. He didn't know how he could get much farther than that. What he wanted to do now was look at the third set of clues.

Jennifer came in, smiled, and looked down at his equation.

"Might be it," she said. "Those last three clues aren't as good as the first ones."

"Let's check out the third set of clues," Longarm said.

Jennifer took them from the envelope where she had kept them. "I haven't even looked at these. I was too confused by the others. Let's hope these are easier." She looked up.

"Oh, I talked to Chief Running Fox. He says he has heard of you; he has heard of Longarm. He remembers other Indians have said that you are a friend to the People, that you know our ways and understand us. He didn't make the connection at first. My grandfather forgets sometimes.

"He says since you are here and have worked so much with other Indian tribes, he wants you to help him solve this problem with the white chief, Godfrey Hamilton. We are to go see my grandfather an hour after the sun sets."

"We're late," Longarm said. "Maybe we should get on our shanks mares and move over that way."

"Are you feeling well enough to go? You've been shot twice in two days."

"Scratches, just scratches. A shot doesn't count unless it hits a bone or something vital. Then it counts."

"Then we'll go. Grandfather was quite insistent."

"Good, we'll get that matter all taken care of and then we can concentrate on the puzzle and the killer. Oh, I think I shouldn't come here too often. I don't want to put you in any danger."

"No danger to me. Let's go."

They walked out the back door, after the inside lamp had been blown out, and were near the edge of town moving toward the Pueblo village when Longarm touched Jennifer's shoulder and they both stopped.

"Somebody's up ahead," he whispered. "Over there on the far side of the street is another person. I'm not sure that this was a good idea coming up here after dark."

Jennifer stared into the darkness.

"I didn't see them. What are we going to do?"

"Wait," Longarm said. "Maybe they'll go away. If they come at us, you stay low. It's me they want, not you."

"Maybe it's nothing, just someone going home."

"No, I've seen them for almost a block. Oh, damn, there's another shadow on this side of the street, and it's coming this way."

Chapter 6

Jennifer Walking Dove stared into the darkness ahead. She hadn't seen the shadows that Longarm spotted.

"Are you sure we're the ones they're interested in?" the Pueblo Indian girl asked softly.

"Absolutely. One behind us has been following us for almost a block. I don't like getting you into this kind of a dangerous situation."

"Longarm, this is my town. I always walk these streets at night. It's probably nothing."

A nighthawk's cry sounded somewhere ahead of them. Jennifer grinned in the darkness. She put one hand to her mouth and realistically imitated the nighthawk. At once the three figures jogged toward them.

"Nothing to worry about," Jennifer said, putting a hand on Longarm's elbow. "Grandfather just sent some people to meet us and be sure that you're safe going to the pueblo."

Longarm grunted in relief. "Good thing I have you along. An Indian could get himself killed that way, sneaking up on a guy in the dark."

Two of the figures ahead of them materialized out of the gloom, spoke in low tones with Jennifer in the Indian tongue, and then all four of them walked quickly toward the village. Two Indians walked behind them twenty yards as a rear guard.

"Glad they knew we were coming," Longarm said.

"Grandfather was concerned when we didn't arrive on time. He always has been a stickler about doing things on time. I think he was the first Indian I ever saw who owned a pocket watch."

Ten minutes later, they climbed the ladder up the side of the first story of the large pueblo complex. On the roof of the first level, they went down another ladder into the first-floor rooms below.

Straw cushions had been placed in the cooking room, and a blaze burned steadily in the corner fireplace, taking the night's chill off the room.

Chief Running Fox sat on one of the straw pillows and watched the fire. He looked up as Jennifer came down the ladder first, followed by Longarm. A slight nod was his only greeting.

Jennifer pointed to the cushion to the left, and she sat on the one between the two men. No words were spoken. Longarm watched the fire of pine branches that burned fiercely. They sat there for five minutes as the fire flamed lower and lower, until it was only bright glowing coals.

Then the same woman he had seen before, wearing a manta, came in with more wood. It had been cut short, and she placed it in the shape of a square, building it a half foot off the coals, then left without a word.

As the flames sprang up into the pitchy pine, Running Fox turned toward Longarm.

"We must find a solution to this problem. There must be no war between our people."

"If the white man must face Pueblo justice, what would the sentence be?" Longarm asked.

Running Fox stared into the fire. One weathered hand came out and motioned as if wiping out the words. "The Pueblo law requires a hand for a hand, a horse for a horse, a life for a life."

"But that is the ages-old tribal law, Chief Running Fox. You are far removed from the simple white-and-black laws of your grandfathers. You have advanced to a much more developed standard; you have progressed in your food raising, in your trading with the other tribes, and in your ways of learning to live near the whites."

"In some ways we have advanced, in some we have not."

"How will it serve both communities if the life-for-a-life law of the Pueblos is carried out?" Longarm asked.

"It will satisfy the boy's family; it will show that the Pueblos are still strong."

"Strong like a small boy shouting to stop the wind or the lightning?"

Chief Running Fox turned and stared at Longarm. "You are a lawman for the Great White Father in Washington."

"Yes, I'm here to protect the Indian wards of the federal government. But I must be fair and impartial to both sides. I understand that Red Feather was not married, so he leaves no widow, no children."

Chief Running Fox nodded.

"That's one problem we don't face. Instead of the law, can we think how the white chief Hamilton can do good for the Pueblo village as payment for the life he accidentally took?"

"What good? We are complete. We sell our goods to other Indians who come from many hundreds of miles to trade. How can a white eye help us?"

"I'm not sure, Chief. I'm trying to find a settlement that would satisfy both the Pueblos and the white chief."

"Grandfather, may I speak?"

The old Indian looked at his granddaughter and nodded sternly, but the hint of a proud smile touched his face.

"Perhaps Dr. Smith could come visit our village once a week. Too many of our babies die. He could help. Some of his medicine can help our people when our own medicine is not strong enough. You have talked about this before, Grandfather. You went to the white doctor twice."

The old Indian nodded slowly.

"That's a start," Longarm said. "The white chief could pay the doctor to make a regular visit to your pueblos if he is agreeable. This is one help. We must work out a number of other ways we can let the white community help your settlement."

They talked for a half hour more but came up with no specific ideas.

Chief Running Fox nodded off a moment, and Jennifer stood. Longarm rose when she did.

"Grandfather, we have stayed too long. I know you are tired. We'll come tomorrow." The old Indian bowed slightly, and his

57

granddaughter and Longarm went up to the roof, then down the outside ladder to the ground.

"A start," Longarm said.

"Yes, but only a start." Jennifer looked behind them when they had left the village. "Don't get jumpy, Longarm. There are two warriors following us, but we probably won't see or hear them. Grandfather doesn't trust you to protect me yet in this strange white-eye village of Taos."

Longarm walked Jennifer to her front door, waited outside until he saw the light come on inside, then told her good night and strolled away. He went a block toward town, then turned and stood in the shadows of a tree and watched. No one moved around him. He was sure that the Indians had headed back to the village. No one else seemed interested in him.

Longarm grinned and went around a block and down the alley, coming to the schoolmarm's house at the back door. He knocked softly, and a moment later the kitchen door opened.

"Longarm?" Jennifer asked from the dark kitchen. He replied and stepped inside and closed the door.

In the front room the blinds were down and two lamps burned on the table, lighting plainly the clues that were supposed to tell them who the embezzler was and probably also who killed Wallace Johnson.

"I'm glad you came back," Jennifer said.

"You told me we had to work on that third set of clues tonight. I enjoy taking orders from pretty girls."

She smiled and pointed at the table. She had laid out the third set of pictures and put away the second.

Longarm stared down at the clues. The first was a drawing of a small black leather case that might be used for many different things. The second was a drawing of a gravestone in a cemetery, the third a picture of a buggy, the next a drawing of a house. Another was a picture of a bottle of cough syrup, and the last was a picture of a thermometer.

"This is it?" Longarm asked. Jennifer stood close to him, staring at the pictures.

She nodded. "Yes. This is the first time I've seen them, too. They look even stranger than the ones in the second group. How can these fit together?"

Longarm shook his head. "An unusual group. The grave marker ties in with the second set, but I don't think that has any bearing on this one. The killer owns a buggy and lives in a house? That is logical, but it could point to a hundred different men."

The two of them stared at the pictures. Jennifer moved them around, changing the positions, then gave up. She turned to Longarm, her dark eyes serious. She put her hands on his shoulders and stared up at him.

"Deputy Custis Long, it's been a strange day. I think it's time that I went to bed." She reached up and kissed his lips lightly. "I'd be ever so pleased right now if you'd come to bed with me."

Longarm put his arms around her shoulders, and she pressed in hard against him.

"Jennifer. I told you that first day this wasn't something that you needed to do. I'm here to find Wallace's killer, and no sacrifices are needed by you."

"I remember, and it's no sacrifice. This is something I've been wanting to do. We've had no fire. This high country gets chilly at night. I need you to help me warm up the bed." She leaned away from him, grinned, and caught his hand.

They carried one lamp into the bedroom. He turned it down low, but she increased the height of the wick.

"I want to see all of you," she said simply and reached up and kissed his lips again, that barely touching, lightning-strike kind of a kiss that sent shivers down his spine.

They sat on the bed, and she turned to him, her voice taking on the sound of a little girl.

"Custis Long, will you please undress me? No one will disturb us here, I guarantee."

He kissed her then, a firm, demanding kiss. She responded, and he knew it would be all right.

An hour later they lay in each other's arms. They had made love twice, and both were resting, planning what would come next.

"You are a tender lover, Custis Long. You know exactly what to do to make me feel so wonderful. You seem to read my mind about when to hurry and when to slow down." She laughed softly and kissed his nose. "Now, Deputy U.S. Marshal Custis Long, I want to do something really crazy, wild, outlandish."

Longarm chuckled. "Any suggestions?"

"Oh, no. I figured you've had a lot more experience than I have and that you'd know something strange and exotic."

He cupped one of her breasts in his hand and caressed it gently. Longarm brightened. "How about standing up? Have you ever made love standing up?"

"Can't be done. Some girls told me they tried. Just wouldn't work. Impossible."

Longarm caught her shoulders and stood her up beside the bed. "Impossible, you say? Good, then we're going to do the impossible."

"You're crazy," Jennifer said, but she laughed delightedly and moved with him. Longarm pressed her against the wall and came up belly-rubbing close.

"See! See how much taller you are. It just will never work. You'd have to stand on your knees, and then you'd be too low." Jennifer giggled. "You are a nut."

"Watch," Longarm said. He took her hands and put them around his neck. "Lace your fingers together and hold on." She did.

"Now lean back against the wall with your back and lift your legs and lock them around my middle."

"Jump up?"

"Any way you can get there."

Jennifer laughed as she got her legs up and around his waist. Then she leaned against the wall with her back and hung on with her hands around his neck.

A moment later, Longarm leaned away from her, adjusted his erection, and then positioned her hips in front of him and slowly drove straight into her heartland.

"Oh, my God!" Jennifer wailed. "I was sure it wasn't possible. Now I see how you're doing it. But we're not really standing up."

"I am," Longarm said. "You started standing up."

"That feels so strange," Jennifer said.

She wailed, and a moment later she climaxed. Her body thrashed from side to side; she brayed, and then the spasms hit her and her whole body vibrated like an out-of-control buggy jolting down a steep hill.

She relaxed for a moment. The most wonderful expression came to her face. "Marvelous, Longarm. I've never felt anything like this before in my whole life! You are a wonder. I can't wait to try this again. Oh, Lord, here it comes again."

Jennifer wailed and gasped, then tore into another set of climaxes that bounced her body against him, that made her cry out in joy and delight, and, in the end, drained her and left her hanging limply onto him.

Longarm had been holding back, and now he began to drive into her with a purpose. His thrusts were short and hard, and she gasped as he slanted deeply into her in this totally new position.

Then he didn't worry if he was hurting her. Nature took over, and his body reacted in the aeons-old dance of love as he spurted a dozen shots into her throbbing, pulsating vagina.

He sagged against her for just a moment, then leaned back, balanced her slender body, and walked to the bed, where he went down on his knees. He eased down sideways onto the bed, with only a small jolt as they both hit the quilts. The boards held and didn't let the springs fall to the floor.

"We did it!" Jennifer said, then kissed him and eased away, resting on the pillows. "That was strange, wild, new, and just a little bit crazy." She snuggled against him. "I wish . . ."

Longarm looked down at her, knowing he shouldn't prompt her. These after lovemaking wishes were usually ones he didn't want to hear.

"I wish we knew right now who it was who killed Wallace. I'd shoot him myself if I knew."

"We'll let the law take care of it, Jennifer. That's why I'm here, remember?"

She snuggled closer and closed her eyes. Slowly she rubbed her breasts against his bare chest. A moment later her hand slipped down to his crotch and found his limp penis.

"Oh, dear, he died down there."

"Needs a little rest, don't you?"

"I don't get a chance like this often. Only once before in my whole life. I'm not going to waste it by sleeping."

She didn't.

By morning, Longarm lay on the bed so exhausted he didn't care if he sprawled there until noon. He had one small nap and woke up when something touched him. He suppressed his usual defensive moves and opened his eyes.

Large, dark eyes swam out of focus in front of his face. Tender lips pressed softly against his, and her natural perfume filled his nostrils.

"Best night I've ever spent," Jennifer whispered.

His arms came around her, and when he pulled her to the bed, he discovered she was still naked.

"Once more?" she asked.

He turned, lifted her, and sat up. He bent and kissed both her breasts and realized they were exactly the right size for her small, slender body.

Longarm reached for his pants. "Hey, lady schoolmarm. Some of us folks have to work during the summer, too. We didn't even get a start on that new set of clues to our killer."

She sat there beside him, her face serious. "Yes. Nor did we even talk about the burial mounds. They must be preserved. No one must touch them. Certainly a horse ranch can't be built on top of them."

"One more job for the U.S. marshal to handle, since it involves wards of the U.S. Government. Now, is there any breakfast in this hotel, or do we go to a café?"

Jennifer Walking Dove giggled and she looked about fifteen. Longarm pulled on his clothes, and by the time he was dressed, Jennifer had a fire going in the kitchen stove and he could smell Arbuckle boiling. She was fast.

When he walked into the kitchen, he saw part of the reason for her speed. Jennifer was still naked.

He patted her bare bottom.

"Oh!" she said.

When she spun around, he caught her and kissed her, then turned her back to the stove.

"Three over easy, heavy on the home-fried potatoes, six flapjacks, hot maple syrup, coffee, and a rasher of bacon."

"How much is a rasher? I've heard the term, but nobody ever tells me how many slices that is."

"At least six."

She put her fists on both hips. "Good. Now I know. For breakfast you get eggs, toast, and coffee. No flapjacks, no bacon, and no home fries."

Longarm grinned. "Great, I'll take it."

Just after eight o'clock that morning, Longarm and Jennifer stepped into the sheriff's office. He reported his talk with

Chief Running Fox and that he hoped there might be a compromise.

"Sure as hell can't turn over Hamilton to the Injuns. I'd never get reelected." Sheriff Nathan Murdock had his town shoes off and massaged his feet. "Now my damned feet hurt. The soles of my feet feel like I walked sixty miles. Never walked even fifty feet yesterday. Damn, guess I'm starting to get old or something."

"Anything new on the Johnson killing?"

The sheriff shook his head. "You got more on that than I do. We don't do much investigating here. You bring in the evidence, and I can collar the gent who done it. Got some boys good with their pieces."

"I'm glad of that, Sheriff. I'll see what I can do." Longarm left the county office feeling overworked. He had counted on some help from the local law. Now he saw why Johnson hadn't wanted to try to have his killer arrested here in Taos and had sent for the marshal.

Longarm and Jennifer stood in the warm sun for a moment, then turned and walked toward the Indian burial mounds. Something felt wrong, damn wrong. Before he got there, he was running, leaving Jennifer to catch up, holding his crossdraw gun leather hard against his hip. He came around the last building that side of the river and looked across. He could see no Pueblo Indian guards.

Longarm splashed across the stream, toward the burial platform that held the body of Red Feather. He still saw no guards. They had been in plain sight before. Where were they?

He ran around the first mound and saw two of the guards tied and gagged near some trees. Longarm ran to them and untied them. They screamed at him and pointed to one of the mounds.

It had been opened. A big pile of dirt showed where the earth had been dug away, exposing a four-foot slash in the mound and at the bottom a hole two feet across.

One of the Pueblo warriors ran to the spot and stared inside. He screamed and shouted something at the other Indian, who turned and ran for the Pueblo buildings.

"Somebody looted the grave," Longarm said. He swore softly as he untied the other two Pueblos, then hurried to the grave. He looked inside and saw in the dim light the skeleton on a mound of dirt. Beside the remains were spears, weapons, and farm tools. On shelves around the side of the grave lay other items the chief would need on his journey into heaven. Near the front of the hole Longarm saw a gleam of something. He covered it with his hand and then slid it into his pocket.

There were more shelves around the tomb, but they were empty. He could see in the dust patterns where something had been removed. He looked in the dirt outside the tomb and found dozens of boot prints.

White men had looted the grave, not Indians. He drew the small object from his pocket and looked at it without letting the Indians see it. It was heavy and bright yellow. Longarm scowled as he realized it was probably pure gold. A small carved figure of some kind.

Somebody had looted the grave and must have stolen all the gold figures there. The Pueblos had never used the soft metal, calling it worthless squaw clay. What were gold figures doing in a Pueblo Indian chief's grave? Just as important, who had looted the grave?

Chapter 7

One of the Pueblo Indian guards near the tombs scowled at
Longarm and pointed across the stream. Jennifer caught up
with Custis and touched his arm.

"You better get back across the Rio Grande, Longarm. You
know how touchy we are about white men on this land. I saw
a runner head for the village. There'll be forty warriors here
in a few minutes."

Longarm pushed the gold figure back into his pocket and
nodded. "Yeah, I reckon you're right. There are boot prints
around here. See if you can find any horse tracks. Should
be some. I'm going to go get a horse so I can follow them,
with or without the Indians' say so. If you can spot any
horseshoe prints leading away from the mound, trail them
off this sacred ground as far as you can, then I won't have
any Indian trouble."

The deputy U.S. marshal turned and walked to the stream,
splashed across it, getting the bottoms of his pant legs wet,
and then jogged toward the livery.

He caught his favorite mare in the corral, saddled her, and
rode back to the river in ten minutes. By then dozens of
Indian men crowded around the open tomb. Chief Running
Fox limped up to the desecrated grave. He spoke with several
of the guards.

Longarm rode to the edge of the stream and looked in the

direction the water flowed. Fifty yards down from the tombs he saw Jennifer waving at him. He rode near her, then crossed the headwaters of the Rio Grande. None of the Indians paid any attention to him.

"I found them," she said. "Grandfather taught me to track. Looks like at least four horses. None of the shoes have any easy-to-see marks. No broken ones, none missing. They head downstream."

He motioned her over beside him and took the gold piece from his pocket. "Ever see anything like that?"

She turned it over and examined it carefully, then shook her head. "It feels heavy enough to be gold. The carving is of some kind of a figure. Look, it has two heads. What is it? Surely it's nothing from the Pueblo tribe."

"I found it at the entrance to the opened tomb. From the dust marks I saw on a shelf inside, I'm afraid many items like this, only much bigger, were stolen from the grave. My guess is that they all were gold like this figure."

Jennifer shook her head. "My people never have used gold. It's considered too soft to be of any value. How would there be any in an ancient Pueblo chief's tomb?"

"How long have your people been in this area?"

"Some say eight hundred years, some say nine hundred years. A long time."

"Did you study in school about the Aztec empire in Mexico?"

"Yes, a little. They lived more than a thousand years ago."

"Their history tells of leaving northern Mexico or the southern United States in the fifteenth century, when your people were in this place. The Aztecs knew much of gold. They developed the use of gold and worked it into pieces of true art. They were good at it. In Aztec ruins they still find gold statues and carvings and delicate castings.

"The only connection I can make is that at some time in their travels in this general part of the world, the Aztecs stopped by at this valley and lived here for a time. They must have been here long enough to teach your early people about gold and the wonders of it in artwork. Maybe the Aztecs even buried one of their own chiefs here with all of his gold knickknacks.

"Why else would there be this gold carving in the opened tomb? Why would the robbers take something from the grave, but not the tools or the items on and around the skeleton of the ancient chief?"

"I'll talk to my grandfather about the ancients."

"Don't mention the gold. We could have a gold rush of white men charging into those tombs and your warriors fighting them. It would be a massacre. Let's keep this little gold piece a secret for now." He took it back from her and put it in his pocket.

Longarm stepped from his mount and hunkered down to study the hoofprints.

"Six horses and heading downstream." He had the Spencer in a boot on his saddle and his .44-40 double-action Colt in his holster. "Time I follow this trail and see what I find at the end."

She touched his shoulder, her face clouded with worry. "Be careful. If they took a lot of gold things, they'll be shooting crazy to keep them and wild to come back and get some more."

Longarm nodded, stepped into the saddle, and walked the mare downstream, checking the hoofprints as he went. He saw Sheriff Murdock limp to the edge of the stream across from the mounds. There was some shouting; then Jennifer ran across the shallow stream, evidently to tell the sheriff what had happened.

Longarm concentrated on his tracking. The trail led into some brush and trees, but he had no trouble following it. A quarter of a mile from the mounds, the prints entered the water. Longarm checked directly across the stream, but found no tracks leaving the water.

He had no idea how old the trail was. Some of the grass had sprung back in place; some hadn't. He rode down the far side of the bank for another quarter of a mile but found no tracks leaving the water.

Longarm crossed the creek and worked his way upstream, watching for any signs that the six mounts had been ridden out of the creek. He found them a hundred yards from where they had entered. The tracks now cut sharply to the west. A half mile later the riders had split up. Three rode on west, and three cut back toward the river.

Longarm couldn't figure it out. Were they lost, or was it some false trail to try to throw him off the scent? A mile ahead, the three riders had made a quarter-mile circle, come back to their previous trail, then shifted fifty feet to the side of the old hoofprints and kept riding in the same direction.

It wasn't a hard job following them. What were they trying to do? The three riders had swung back west again, climbed a small ridge, and headed down the other side.

Longarm sat his bay on the ridge and scanned the valley in front of him. It was no more then half a mile long, with a green line of brush marking a wandering creek that wound down from the head of the valley. The mountain meadow spread less than five hundred yards wide.

Most of the country here, and that he had been riding through, bristled with ponderosa. Not a solid growth, but enough to hold the dirt on the slopes. Toward the head of this valley stood a grove of blue spruce. Usually they grew at higher altitudes. Longarm judged that he had ridden a thousand feet downhill from Taos, which had to be at least seven thousand feet in altitude. That made this valley a little low for a grove of blue spruce.

Just over the slope, he paused and checked the valley again. Dots in the grassy areas of the valley floor began to move. Range cattle. He looked at the head of the valley. This time he spotted a small streamer of smoke rising well above the blue spruce before it blew to his left. A fire, which could mean a cabin or a ranch house, or even an open camp, but in any case it should mean the end of the trail.

Longarm changed directions, ignored the prints he'd been following, and rode over the ridge to be out of sight of the grove of spruce. Then he climbed along the slope, up the ridge, to get closer to the camp and what he hoped was the spot where the grave robbers had come to roost.

It was slower going on the side of the slope. He rode down to the narrow valley, and kicked the bay into a lope for half a mile until the valley petered out into a rocky spine. Longarm turned up the slope again to the ridge and looked over.

He could see the grove more plainly now. He judged he was about a quarter of a mile from the stand of spruce. Between him and the smoke the cover was sparse. A sprinkle of ponderosa lifted a hundred, some a hundred and fifty, feet into the air.

The trouble was there weren't enough of the trees to hide him, even if he worked on foot toward the smoke.

Longarm concentrated on the smoke path. Through the ponderosa he could spot the dark outline of a building, a cabin of sorts. The trees hid everything else. He didn't know if there were horses there, and if so, how many. How many men were in the place? Had they brought the loot here or was this a wayside stop in a run for Santa Fe?

Longarm grunted as he stepped off the bay. He tied her where she could find some grass, then checked the top of the valley below him. It swept into a rocky ledge, then angled to the left up another narrow gully toward what he figured must be a lesser peak along the range.

Just this side of the rocky ledge grew a good cover of brush and small trees. Some ancient landslide must have toppled all of the older trees and provided fresh growing soil for the new seeds. It was his safe path of concealment down to the cabin.

Longarm mounted and rode as close to the brushy slide as he could get and still have cover. Then he tied the bay, took the Spencer, pushed two extra tubes of ammunition inside his shirt, and headed for the brush.

It took him twenty minutes to work down the slope and hit the first of the blue spruce. The trees were half-grown, maybe a foot through, and closely spaced. Almost no underbrush grew around them. Longarm picked his way through until he could see the log cabin ahead. It had been built from the spruce in the grove, had a window in the front, a sloping roof on its one-story structure, and looked as if it might have four rooms.

To the left, three horses stood tied to a rail. There was no corral, no pens, no barn or place for the stock, and no bunkhouse. Not even a well. The small stream that chattered a hundred feet over must have provided water.

He was as close as he could get from this side. The window commanded a view of the ground in front and some to the side. Slowly, and without making a sound, Longarm worked around the cabin until he was at the side. This wall had no window. He was about to leave the last cover and sprint for the cabin, when he heard the slam of a spring-loaded screen door.

A man came out what must have been a back door, walked a dozen feet into the woods, and urinated. He looked like a cowboy, had a tall hat, sideburns, jeans, and a blue shirt. He wore no neckerchief or gunbelt.

When the stranger vanished back into the house, Longarm held the rifle at port arms and jogged for the side of the cabin. He made it with no outcry. He figured they would not have a guard out. Now he moved cautiously toward the rear of the cabin, where he thought there must be a back door.

At the edge of the rough logs with their notched ends, he peered around and saw the rear of the structure. It had an opening set in it, with a screen door and a solid door beyond that. There was no rear window. The door handle rattled and the inner door opened.

"Dammit to hell, why it got to be me all the time? Yeah, yeah, I'll go. Best be a damn lot of cash in this for all the trouble." When the man finished talking, he was past the screen and let it slam. A pile of sawed and split firewood lay against the far side of the building, under the overhang, partly, Longarm imagined, to keep it out of the rain and winter snow and partly so it would be close.

The man looked young, wore a gun, gray pants, and a mashed-in-crown wide-brimmed hat. He knelt at the pile of wood to fill up his arms.

Longarm covered the distance in three silent strides. The side of the Colt slammed downward across the side of the man's head, and he groaned and slumped on the wood he'd been trying to pick up.

Longarm grabbed him under both arms and dragged him past the back door and out of sight, around the side of the cabin. He bound the man's hands in back of him, lifted the six-gun from the stranger's holster, and pushed it into his own belt. By the time he had the man's ankles tied together, he'd come to.

Longarm clamped a hand over the cowboy's mouth and rested the muzzle of his Colt against the grave robber's forehead.

"We're going to have a nice quiet talk, understand? You make any loud noise and my trigger finger is going to get jumpy and pull hard. You savvy?"

The young man nodded.

"How many men inside?"

Longarm took his hand away from the kid's mouth. He swallowed, and his eyes rolled from side to side; then he frowned.

"Don't kill me, just don't kill me. Two others. Shaky and Wild Bill. Who are you?"

"Friend of the family. You have the gold from the grave inside?"

"Hell no, Karl took it. Didn't trust us. Said we was decoys."

"What's your name?"

"Handy Prescott."

"You dug into the burial mound?"

"Yeah, after we clobbered them Injuns. They was easy. They figured nobody would bother them."

"This Karl's idea?"

"Hell no. Karl ain't that smart. He's just following orders."

"Who gave the orders?"

"Damned if I know. Karl didn't tell nobody. Hired us out of the saloon, ten bucks a day. Nothing honest pays that much."

"Where do you go from here?"

"Didn't tell us. Said he'd be over to pay us tomorrow."

"Karl has all the gold?"

"Yeah. I figure about twenty of them figures. Damn heavy, that gold."

"Where did Karl go?"

"Didn't tell us."

Longarm brought down his kerchief, rolled it into an inch-wide band, and tied it securely over Handy's mouth and around his head.

"Stay quiet and you stay alive."

Longarm lifted away from the kid he figured to be more like eighteen than twenty, and stepped to the back door. He had checked the kid's .45 and found five rounds loaded. He set the rifle against the wall, then fisted the .45 lefty. He cocked the hammers of both hand weapons and pulled open the screen. In one swift movement he turned the knob and kicked open the heavy wooden door. Both his six-guns came up, covering the room.

He saw one man near the fire.

"Where the hell you been? Fire almost—"

The speaker turned then and saw a stranger and grabbed for his revolver. Longarm's first shot, from his own .44-40, lanced through the man's chest from side to side, churning up all sorts of damage to his heart, passing on through a failing lung, and

71

exiting between ribs and into the wood-burning kitchen range. He slumped to the floor.

"What the hell?" A voice boomed from behind the log partition that divided the cabin into two rooms.

Longarm dove to the left as he saw a big man with a sawed-off shotgun come through the opening between the two rooms. The scattergun exploded, and Longarm fired with both hands at the gunner in the doorway. The heavy lead slugs from the scattergun blasted through the space where Longarm had been, thudding into the wall. The roar of the shotgun blast and the two six-gun shots filled the room with a rolling thunder.

The big man had been striding forward. The force of the two big lead slugs stopped his advance. He teetered on his feet a moment, then dropped the shotgun and crumpled to the floor with a round in his left lung and another through his nose. The head-shot slug had slanted upward into his brain and chopped up a dozen vital functions. He was dead before he hit the floor.

Longarm checked the back room. No one else was there. A quick inspection of the cabin showed that the men hadn't been there long. They had one day's supply of food and a frying pan. Longarm dragged the bodies out of the cabin and brought Handy around.

"They drew down on me but didn't quite make it," Longarm said.

Handy looked at the larger of the dead men. His face turned white, and he bent over and threw up.

It was a half hour later by the time Longarm had tied the two bodies on their horses, mounted the kid and tied his hands to the saddle horn, and roped his feet together under the horse's belly. He tied lead lines to the two packhorses, and another to Handy's mount, and moved out, making better time than on his trip in.

He found the place where the trail split and this time followed the other three sets of prints.

"How do you do that?" Handy asked. "I can't see no damn trail."

"You don't know what to look for."

The track wound back toward the South Road out of Taos, which ended in Santa Fe. Once they got to the road, the other three grave robbers had ridden faster to the south.

Longarm almost missed the turnoff. The three mounts had taken a faint trail to the left, into a more heavily wooded area. The ponderosa were plentiful here, and twice Longarm had to backtrack to untangle the lead line horses where they had gone around a tree on the wrong side.

A half mile off the road, the trail became fainter yet, and Longarm started to wonder if he had missed a turnoff. Fifty feet farther on he spotted a cabin ahead. It hunkered against an upthrust and a rocky cliff that seemed to rise up from nothing.

Longarm knew that upthrusts of hard rock that had lasted down through the centuries were sometimes a harbinger of a hard-rock gold vein. Some ambitious prospector had put up a cabin, he figured, then tried digging into the cliff to find his fortune.

The cabin had half fallen in, but three horses grazed on long pickets in a grassy place near a small creek nearby.

Longarm tied his horses well back and put the gag back around Handy's mouth. He let the kid off the horse and tied him to a tree, then looked around. No smoke came from the rock-and-mortar chimney. It was past midday, but Longarm told himself he wasn't hungry. He had to recover the gold and hush up the story, or it would be all over Taos and nobody would be able to stop a battle to rip open the remaining burial mounds.

For fifteen minutes, he watched what was left of the front door to the cabin. The wooden panel had been replaced with a blanket that hung at a crazy angle dictated by the overhead beams, which had shifted.

Windows? Longarm made a swift, yet silent, trip around the cabin, staying out of sight. There was one window that had long ago lost its glass. It was now covered with a piece of cardboard. The place had only one door. That made it simpler. For a moment Longarm wished he had one of the army's small hand bombs. He could light the fuse and toss it inside, let it blast the place apart, then go in and pick up the gold and leave the splattered remains of the grave robbers looking for their own final resting place.

The use of the small grenades by deputies was frowned upon by the U.S. marshals. Billy Vail wouldn't care if he didn't know. Longarm sighed. He had to go down there and roust them out. No time to play the waiting game. The old trick of picking them off one at a time when they came outside to relieve themselves wouldn't work. He didn't have time.

He was ready to start working toward the side of the cabin when he heard the deadly sound of a weapon cocking behind him.

"Jeeze but you're sloppy. You didn't even check me for a hideout or a knife."

Longarm turned slowly, his hand well away from his weapon.

Handy grinned at him from six feet away, a two-shot derringer aimed at Longarm's chest.

"Jeez, for a deputy U.S. goddam marshal you sure as hell are sloppy."

Chapter 8

Deputy U.S. Marshal Custis Long had dropped to one knee for a last look at the cabin ahead before he made his move. Now he watched the kid with a big grin and a derringer aimed at him from six feet behind.

"Damn bad work by you, Marshal. You shoulda knowed better. Now just ease that big six-gun out of leather, so I don't have to shoot you dead. I can't miss with this hideout at two yards. We both know that."

"You must want me to stand up first to make a better target," Longarm asked. He waited, where he knelt, his right hand near his right boot on the ground.

"Well, now that you mention it, that will make a bigger body to hit at." Handy Prescott grinned. "Yeah, Marshal, you just stand yourself up."

Longarm lifted slowly, moving his weight to his left foot. Then, as his knee straightened, he took a short step forward with his left foot, to get his balance.

At the same time his left foot moved, his right hand shot forward in an underhanded throw. The boot knife from his right boot didn't have time to turn. It drove forward flat and even, and just as the surprised Handy saw the movement, he lifted the derringer but didn't have time to pull the trigger. The four-inch blade drove into the grave robber's chest, slightly below the heart.

Handy groaned and his eyes went wide. He sank to both knees, dropping the hideout, his hands closing around the pearl handle of the knife, holding it in place. His face paled; then without a word he fell forward on his face, ramming the blade deeper into his chest.

Longarm drew his Colt and eased the kid over on his back. The half-inch-wide blade must have sliced through one of the major tubes taking blood from his heart. He died in seconds. Longarm drew the blade out, wiped it off on Handy's pants, and pushed it back into the slot in his right boot.

Handy had been right. He hadn't even considered that the young man would have a knife or a hideout gun. Longarm dismissed the episode and turned back to the target.

Inside the tumbledown cabin he expected he'd find the other three grave robbers, led by Karl. He looked over the place again, then nodded. In a nearby ponderosa pine stump, a long-downed tree, he found what he wanted. The sap of the tree had run down into the stump, and as the other wood rotted, the sap turned into what woodsmen call pitch.

It's the hardened sap that's the solid equivalent of turpentine and burns just as well. Wet pitch wood from a winter water-soaked pine stump can be kicked out and will burn instantly at the touch of a match. Longarm found enough of the hard pitch wood for what he wanted and carried a bundle of it in one hand as he worked around to the blind side of the cabin and hurried toward the blank log wall.

No one stopped him or called out an alarm. The grave robbers inside must have felt secure. Longarm took a half-inch-wide stick of the pitch a foot long and cut turned-out grooves in it, making it look like a small feather. He did the same with three more of the sticks, then carried them along the wall until he could reach around and lay them directly under the folded-over bottom of the blanket that served as the cabin door.

He struck a match and lit one of the pitch fuzz sticks. When it was burning intensely, he lay it next to the other two and piled another pitch stick on top of it, edging it up to the blanket. Then he pulled back so he was away from the doorway but could see it plainly. He held one six-gun in each hand now and quietly cocked both weapons.

The pitch sticks burned fiercely, setting the blanket on fire. Cloth burns slowly and causes a lot of smoke. It took nearly five minutes for the smoke seeping inside the cabin to be noticed.

A loud voice bellowed a question. Another voice shot back some words Longarm couldn't understand. Then one man rushed out past the half-burned blanket door rubbing his eyes and coughing. He didn't see Longarm.

"Get out of there before you get smoke fever!" the man outside called.

Two more men charged past the burning blanket and looked around.

"Who in hell?" one screeched. He looked directly at Longarm and started to draw his revolver, but a round from Longarm's Colt caught him in the belly and he sat down suddenly, holding his gut and screaming.

The other two men darted in opposite directions. Longarm fired at the closest, missed and stabbed a second shot at him that hit the man in the leg. He rolled behind some brush and a pine tree. The third man vanished in the brush.

Longarm hunkered down behind the wall. He was covered from both the gunmen, but he had no field of fire at them. He eased forward, leaned outward to show himself, then pulled back at once.

A revolver barked across the small clearing, and the slug hit the log cabin near where Longarm had shown himself.

The deputy marshal took another look from ground level and saw the white smoke that marked the spot from where the gunman had fired.

Longarm put three rounds into the area, one in the middle and one on each side. He heard no screech of pain.

"Who the hell are you?" The voice came from the man Longarm figured he'd hit in the leg.

"Who the hell is asking?"

"You don't know us, then why you burning us out?" It was the same voice, which was now edged with pain.

"The gold, why else?"

"You gut-shot Karl," a new voice said from the far brush. "He's good as dead. Why don't we split up the gold and ride for Santa Fe? Hell, nobody ever know the difference."

"What about the guy in town who hired you?"

"Hell, Karl said the old geezer who hired us didn't know for sure anything was in the graves. Said it was a gamble and

77

outside chance might be something there. The towner didn't know for sure."

"How much gold you get?" Longarm asked.

"Seventy, maybe eighty pounds. Worth a hell of a lot of cash. Now, tell us, who are you?"

"I'm a deputy U.S. marshal and both you boys are gonna hang. Toss out your weapons and you'll have a chance."

Longarm heard a lot of swearing from the far robber.

"Don't try for your horses. They're on my side of the cabin. I'll shoot them dead before you can get to them."

"Oh, damn. This one was supposed to be so easy." The voice had more pain in it now. It came from the man closest.

"Hell, I'm coming in. Can't hang a man for a robbery. I know that much. Besides, you winged me in the leg and I think it broke a bone."

Longarm waited, let the silence string out.

"You hear me, Marshal? Said I want to surrender." A six-gun sailed out of the brush and landed a dozen feet from the cabin. "I'm coming out now. Don't shoot."

Longarm waited. A man stood slowly, from some brush that was closer than where the lawman had guessed the man to be hiding. He crawled toward the cabin. He had both his hands up and limped forward. When he was fully in the open, he called again.

"I'm giving up, Marshal, coming in."

The words had just left his mouth when three shots sounded from the far brush. The rounds slammed through the hushed quiet of the high-country pine woods. The grave robber giving up screamed and staggered forward a step; then one more round caught him in the back, and he jolted forward and crumpled in a lifeless mass.

The echo of the four shots rippled back down the small valley. Longarm turned toward the horses. The gunman wouldn't need them. He had silenced his fellow robber; now all he had to do was fade into the brush and trees and walk back to town.

Longarm bent low and ran past the far end of the cabin. He sprinted ten yards to the edge of the clearing and dove into the brush. He drew no shots.

Longarm lay in the brush, grass, and pine needles listening. He'd played this game with experts, Indian experts. It was less than two minutes before he heard movement. The man was ahead and slightly to the right, close to the clearing but moving around it in the other direction, heading for the road.

The lawman reloaded his Colt and holstered it. He moved forward after the robber. He traveled ten feet without making a sound, then stopped and listened.

A small branch broke ahead, followed by a grunt of pain.

Longarm worked forward. The robber was trying to play Indian, by not making any sound, which meant he would have to move extremely slow.

Five minutes later, Longarm slid into place behind a two-foot-thick ponderosa and peered around it. Twenty feet ahead a man eased one foot to the ground, then stepped forward with the other. As he did, he turned and looked behind him.

Longarm shot him in the right leg. The robber bellowed in pain, stumbled and fell forward, and his own six-gun dropped to the ground and fired harmlessly.

"Don't reach for the piece or you're a dead man," Longarm brayed at the killer.

The man turned a glowering face toward Longarm.

"You shot me without warning!"

"How much warning did you give your buddy back there in the clearing before you murdered him? What's your name?"

"Phil Noonan."

Longarm bandaged the killer's leg wound so he wouldn't bleed to death, checked him carefully for any hideout or knife, then marched Noonan back to the cabin, where the blanket still smoldered. Longarm tied up the wounded killer, then checked on the gut-shot outlaw called Karl. He was dead.

In the dark, smoky cabin, Longarm found the gold. Twenty pieces all laid out on a rotting table. Some were no larger than the one in his pocket; some must have weighed ten pounds.

He packed them in saddlebags and carried them outside one at a time. He figured there were well over a hundred pounds of gold artifacts.

Longarm took stock. He had five dead bodies, one wounded man, and a hundred pounds of Indian artifacts made of pure gold. First he had to hide the artifacts, where they'd stay until the right time came to return them to Chief Running Fox. The deputy marshal made two trips. He carried three of the saddlebags at a time into the heavy brush, pacing off the distance, remembering the spot by the huge ponderosa pine and the three sister pines nearby.

He kicked the pine-needle mulch away from the ground and clawed out more with his hands until he had a small hole a foot deep and three feet long. In it he put the saddlebags and then covered them with the mulch and some brush so the spot was well hidden.

Back at the fallen-down cabin, Longarm made sure the last of the smoldering blanket and his small pitch fire were out, then brought up the horses and tied the bodies on. One last task.

Longarm squatted down beside the grave robber he had tied up and touched the man's right leg where the bullet wound showed red through the bandage.

"Hey, that hurts."

"Not half as bad as a hangman's noose is gonna hurt, Noonan. Who hired you to dig into those Indian mounds?"

"Karl did. I just rode in from the north. I was having a beer in a saloon. He said I could make ten dollars for two days work. I signed on."

"Karl wasn't smart enough to plan this job. Who was he working for?"

"He never said. I didn't ask. Ten bucks is more cash than I've seen in a month."

"Not much of a cash haul to be hung for, Noonan."

"I won't hang."

"You're betting your life on it. Let's get back to town." Longarm boosted the wounded man onto his horse, then tied his feet together under the mount's belly. She skittered around a few minutes, then got used to the new belly rope and settled down.

It took them two hours to get back to town. The lead line with six horses on it and five bodies caused a stir, and by the time Longarm reined up in front of the courthouse, there were twenty men, women, and children following the grisly procession. A deputy ran for the sheriff, who limped out. He used a cane today.

"You again?"

"These are the six men who dug into the Indian burial mounds. They resisted arrest. This live one is Phil Noonan.

He killed one of his buddies when he tried to surrender. I'm charging him with murder."

The sheriff instructed his men to take the living robber into the jail and sent the rest to the undertaker.

Sheriff Murdock motioned Longarm to one side, away from the crowd. He spoke softly. "I hear there was some looting from the grave, is that right? These fellas steal some things?"

"They did, and I recovered them. Indian artifacts. I'll be returning them to the owners at the proper time. Right now it's too touchy a matter. Oh, Noonan shouldn't be allowed to talk to anyone. He might have some wild stories about what was in that tomb. Wouldn't want anything like that to get out and stir up the town."

The old lawman stared at Longarm a moment, then nodded. "That's for damn sure, Longarm. Don't want this blown up any more than it is. Now, my other damn big problem. How the hell we gonna keep Hamilton from getting himself killed by the Indians?"

"I'm working on it, Sheriff. Might have a couple of ideas."

"Anything new on the Johnson killing?"

"Working on that, too. Seems like all of a sudden I have a half dozen problems. Which I better get back to. I'll sign a complaint against that prisoner. I want him charged with murder. When will the circuit court judge be through here?"

The two walked to the courthouse and got the paperwork done. The judge wasn't due for three weeks yet. Longarm said he'd leave a deposition in the case and headed back to the hotel.

He washed up, shaved, and put on clean clothes. Then he had an early supper. Next on his agenda was a small Indian lady and her dining-room table full of clues.

It was nearly dark as Longarm walked along the street from the hotel. He had just stepped down from the board-walk in front of the Anderson Haberdashery when a rifle shot blasted ahead of him and from across the street. The round ripped through his flat-crowned brown Stetson. The deputy marshal zigzagged across the alley and skidded to a stop behind the protective wall of the building across the way. He peered out from the corner but saw only a white puff of smoke, blowing away from the top of the Silver Dollar Saloon.

There had been only one shot. The building stood alone. Anyone on the roof would have had to go down the back, probably on a ladder. Longarm raced across the street, his six-gun in hand, and sprinted alongside the saloon, through an empty lot to the back of the building. He saw no one on the ladder.

A flash of white caught his eye as someone vanished into the back of the next building to the north. A vacant lot came first, then the back door of the Hawkins Hardware.

Longarm raced to the store and inside. He was in a large room filled with backstock, kegs of nails, boxes and stacks of all kinds of merchandise. A swinging door led into the main store. He bolted through the door and came face-to-face with a man wearing a visor and with a stack of empty boxes in his hands.

"Yep, how can I help you?"

"Mr. Hawkins?"

"True enough, that's me. What do you need today?"

"Did a man just come through here?"

"Nope, not from the front nor the back. Business is a little off. I'd have noticed."

Longarm raced back through the swinging doors and saw the rear door of the stockroom just closing. The bushwhacker had hidden among the merchandise, then escaped out the back door.

The deputy sprinted for the door and pushed it open. When he looked down the alley, all he saw was the whorehouse next door and a donkey tied to the rail in back. On the small back dock by the door he saw two white sticks, flat and thin. They were about six inches long and half an inch wide. They were rounded on both ends and had been sanded smooth. Strange. He picked them up and put them in his pocket. They hadn't been there when he went into the store.

Longarm ran to the bawdy house and in the back door. A woman wearing only a skirt and smoking a thin, long cigar stared at him.

"Most gents come in the front door," she said. "Hell, I'll make an exception for you."

"Where's the man who just ran in here out of breath?"

"They all get short on breath when they see my titties."

"This one might have had a rifle."

82

She shook her head, then her whole torso, so her breasts swung delightfully. "Nope, didn't see him. Can I interest you in a delicious bite or two?" She walked toward him, her breasts doing a practiced, fancy little dance all their own.

"Maybe later. I should check every room."

"Last gent who tried that damn near got his face blown off with a derringer. Don't think he's stopped running yet."

"You must have seen him come in the back door."

"I get paid not to see nothing. Especially I don't tell lawmen what I see. You're that deputy U.S. marshal, I'd wager. The girls said you was handsome enough to do a free one for. But like I say, I didn't see nothing."

Longarm sniffed, moved toward the back door, and sniffed again. There was that same smell. He'd had a whiff of it in the hardware store. The smell was familiar, but he couldn't pin it down. Not a perfume, not fancy cologne. An industrial smell? Coal dust? No. Grease, smoke, turpentine? A paint smell? He voted no on each one.

The whore facing him, now only six feet away, smiled. "You're changing your mind. You want to see the rest of the pretty package. I take care of myself. No fat or flab, and a nice tight, cozy pussy that'll eat you alive." She stepped out of her skirt, spread her legs, and humped her hips forward.

"Nice. Now put your clothes on. I never pay for pussy. If you change your mind about seeing that guy who busted in here, you send a note to me at the hotel or the sheriff's office. The varmint has killed at least one man, and he just tried to bushwhack me with a rifle. When you change your mind about describing him to me, you get in touch."

Longarm winked at her, turned, and left the place by the back door. The mule was gone. He shrugged. The whore must have seen the man. If only she would forget her whore's code of honor and tell him, it would be a big break.

Ten minutes later, Longarm walked up to the back door of the schoolmarm's house. It was almost dark. He knocked. The door swung wide almost at once.

Jennifer Walking Dove stood waiting for him. She had her short hair combed neatly and wore a Indian dress made of soft doeskin with dozens of small patterns sewn on it in tiny colored beads.

She smiled at him. "I'm glad you came. I wanted to show you my ceremonial dress. Do you like it?"

"Nice," he said, realizing it was the same term he had used when he looked at the naked whore. "Is this a special occasion?"

Jennifer smiled. "It might be, who knows? I had some ideas about the clues. Would this be a good time to go over them?"

She caught his hand and led him into the kitchen and then to the dining-room table. The clues were spread out as before, with only the third set showing.

She had put the pictures of the small black case, the grave marker, and the buggy in a row. "I was thinking that maybe our man is the undertaker. I've seen our digger man with his kit of materials he takes on house calls. You know, when the family wants the body kept at home until the burial. He takes things in a little black suitcase. I guess it's bigger than this one. But he's very much associated with grave markers. Fact is, our undertaker also is a stonecutter for the markers.

"Then the picture of the house for when he goes to the house to fix up the deceased so he looks nice for the funeral." She turned to Longarm, her dark eyes eager for some response.

"Possible. But what about the buggy, the cough syrup, and the thermometer? How would they fit that scene?"

Jennifer shook her head. "I didn't say my idea was perfect. Just the best I've come up with so far."

Longarm stared at the clues to the puzzle. For just a moment he wondered if the smell he had had a whiff of could be tied to any of these clues. He looked at them for five minutes, then pushed the smell aside. He had to identify the smell first, then he'd have a chance to make it fit in.

He took the two small, flat sticks from his pocket. Had they been dropped outside the hardware store by the ambusher in a big rush, or were they something else? He wasn't sure. He laid them on the table and wrote a note about the smells he had experienced twice now. He put the note beside the pictures.

It had to be here. It had to be staring him right in the face, but for the life of him he couldn't tie it down. What in hell was it he had missed?

Chapter 9

The short Indian maid and the long, tall Virginia-bred deputy U.S. marshal stared at the pictures until their eyes burned in their sockets. She talked him into staying the night, and they had a slap-and-tickle time until Longarm called a halt and opined that they better get some sleep. The next day they had to face down Grandpa Chief Running Fox with a set of compromises good enough to convince the tribal council to let the white man live who had killed Red Feather.

In the morning, after they'd had a quick breakfast and put on some clean clothes, Longarm and Jennifer Walking Dove arrived at the seven-level pueblo. It was before eight o'clock, and the apartments were busy, with many Indian men, women, and children moving around.

Chief Running Fox had a different apartment this time for them to use for their conference. They climbed to the very top of the adobe-and-pole building and stepped through a roof-level door made in the shape of a T. The three-room unit was like the others, but this one had one large white-eye chair with soft cushions.

Chief Running Fox sat there and nodded. "Old bones like chair sitting better than floor sitting," he said to explain the modern convenience. Then he frowned. "You have an answer for our problem with the white chief who killed Red Feather?"

Longarm had pondered on it all the way to the village. He had worked out several ideas. Now he pitched out the first one to see how the Indian chief would react.

"I have seen your men and women working in their fields. They use sticks to dig the soil. What you must have are two steel plows, each to be pulled by a horse or mule. You have the mules. The white chief will purchase and give to you two of the steel walking plows. They will dig the soil deeper, make a better seedbed, and mean a larger yield of crops from the same fields."

Longarm and Jennifer sat on the heavy pillows on the floor, and he saw her nod in approval of the idea.

"Along with the plow and the two harnesses for the horses to use to pull the plow, you need many more tools. I'd suggest twenty-five long-handled shovels, twenty-five rakes, and twenty-five hoes to help cut the weeds from around your crops. These tools will make the farming work much easier and help you produce better crops."

Longarm watched the old Indian. Slowly he nodded. "Yes, tools will be good. Help us do better work. I like the plow."

Longarm went over the list he had put together. "I suggest that the white chief also furnish the Pueblos with twenty-five wooden barrels that hold thirty gallons each. These can be sawn in half and used in the rooms here for storage of corn and beans and other crops. They will keep longer in the wooden barrels."

The Indian chief nodded. "I have seen the wooden barrels. They are good."

"The final suggestion I have is that the white doctor from Taos be hired by the white-eye chief to come to the pueblo one day each week and help your new mothers, and your old women, and anyone else who has a health problem that Pueblo medicine will not cure. I know, I know, there are not many, but some of your people the white-eye medicine can help, and this will be beneficial to all the members of your tribe."

The old Indian frowned and turned to his granddaughter. They spoke rapidly in a dialect that Longarm didn't understand. It was a small argument of sorts, and when Jennifer looked at Longarm, she lifted her brows.

"My grandfather is not entirely happy with the white-eye doctor idea. He will present it to the tribal council in the *kiva* as soon as they assemble. That is a meeting neither of us can attend.

"Sometimes if we sit close to the big *kiva,* we can hear the talk and even see the smoke."

Longarm tried to read the mood and the position of the old chief. He had won on the plow and tools; he needed something that would clinch the proposal. "One last offer," Longarm said. He had saved it as a kind of insurance in case something else was vetoed out of hand. Now he used it. "The Pueblo raise horses to trade with other warriors of the People. You have been a trade center here for hundreds of years, trading horses and your corn and pumpkins and beans. It is my suggestion that you now start a small herd of white man's buffalo, the beef cattle. I suggest that the white chief give to the Pueblo ten brood cows and one prime bull to start a herd. The cows will calve each year. The female calves should be saved to be brood cows, the male calves cut and raised as steers for butchering. Also the white-eye chief will bring within a week ten steers three-years-old or more, ready for butchering, so the Pueblo will have a continuing supply of meat."

The usually impassive old Indian smiled and nodded. "Yes, I have eaten this white man's buffalo. The meat is soft and not as tasty as buffalo or elk, but it will keep our people fed." He frowned and rubbed his forehead; then his face turned to a smile. "I will take your offer to the council. We will probably talk for many hours."

"We'll take a walk, Grandfather, perhaps go back to town," Jennifer said. She touched the old man's arm as she rose and motioned for Longarm to come with her. Outside on the patio-like roof of the apartments below, they looked over the landscape. The hills were heavily timbered in spots with ponderosa and on the higher levels with blue spruce and Douglas fir. On some of the mountains there were only scattered trees and brush. Some nearby slopes had been stripped bare of all wood for fires.

"Will the council talk take a long time?" Longarm asked.

"Something this complicated could take all day and half the night."

"Can I see the *kiva?*"

"No, it is sacred ground. But I can tell you about it. The *kiva* here is dug into the ground in the center of the lowest level of

87

the seven-story pueblo. This is to protect it. This placement was first done when the Spanish were here. It helped us to conceal our rituals from their eyes.

"This *kiva* is twenty feet long and ten feet wide and is the tribe's one ceremonial room. It has been made with stone blocks fitted to form the walls, then plastered with adobe mortar to form a solid, secure structure. Stones were used on the floor as well, flat thin ones usually and with adobe mortar lathered between them.

"In the center of our *kiva* there was dug a fire pit. At the far end of the room a low masonry shelf was built to hold sacred artifacts and objects. The *kachina house* is an area behind this shelf where the ceremonial masks are all hung when not being used. Actually this is little more than a narrow niche in the wall to hold the masks.

"At the same end of the room, the *sipapu* is built into the floor. This is the most sacred part of the *kiva*. It is a cavity in the floor a foot deep and ten inches wide that is usually covered with a piece of smooth pine or cottonwood plank. In the middle of this plank is a four-inch-square hole that is fitted with a wooden plug.

"This plug represents the spot where the Pueblo People emerged from the center of the earth to live on the surface. This plug is the symbolic contact between the natural and the supernatural worlds for the Pueblo Indians."

"Is this also the place where the council meets to discuss problems and pound out laws and rules, and settlements with white eyes who violate the Pueblo law?" Longarm asked.

"It is. Sometimes the talk goes on for hours. Any of the elders of the tribe who want to talk about a subject being considered is allowed to speak for as long as each man wishes."

They worked their way down the ladders and rooftops to the plaza in front of the two apartment structures.

"What do you think of the suggested settlement for the death of Red Feather?" Longarm asked.

Jennifer frowned, then looked up at him. "It's generous; I'm sure much more than Chief Running Fox expected. He's used to being cheated by the whites. He was pleased by your offer. What I can't figure out is how you talked Godfrey Hamilton into doing all of this."

"I haven't. If the Indians accept the offer, it will be binding on him unless he wants to leave town and forfeit all of his goods and property here. He'll accept it. He has no other choice. It's that, or he can try to run, or he can choose to toast over a Pueblo camp fire head-down."

Jennifer looked up quickly. "Oh, our people don't do that anymore."

Longarm grinned. "We both know that, but we want to be sure that Godfrey Hamilton doesn't know it." They looked at each other and laughed.

"Oh, you didn't mention that small gold item you found in the tomb. Should Grandfather know about that?"

"Not yet. There were more gold items, many of them. I got them back from the grave robbers and have them hidden. When we get the death payments agreed upon, I'll go with you and one trusted warrior and your grandfather to reopen the tomb and put the gold items back. We don't want any word of this to leak out to the white population, or the men in town will storm those graves and your men will respond and we'll have a bloodbath. We can't allow that to happen."

"Oh, I agree. But didn't one of the white robbers live? Won't he spread the word?"

"I've told the sheriff to keep him under a tight lockup. Anything he says will be discredited."

"But didn't someone hire the men?"

"The robbers told me the man who hired them did it on a guess, on speculation. I'm sure he doesn't know what the men found in the tombs. They hadn't had time to report to him before I hit them."

"So who hired them?"

"That's another small problem we need to work on." They walked back toward town. "Did that part of a night's sleep help untangle any of those clues to Wally's killer for you?" Longarm asked.

She shook her head. "Not a one. I'm still stumped."

"Me, too, but I've got another clue for you. It's a smell. I noticed it when I chased the man who bushwhacked me with the rifle in town yesterday. It's a strange smell. I've been around it before, but I can't quite pin it down. When I figure out that smell, we'll have our killer."

He tried to describe it to her but knew he wasn't using quite the right words.

They stopped at a small café on Main Street and had coffee and cinnamon rolls.

"We know the killer is a man with money, lives in town, evidently strikes swiftly, and doesn't like the church," Jennifer said. "The last set of clues showed us he had a small black suitcase, a grave marker, a buggy, and a house." Jennifer shook her head, and her short black hair bounced.

"I still can't make anything out of it. Now we add this certain strange smell." She threw up her hands in frustration. "It could be a dozen different men."

"The easiest way to pick out candidates is still the rich clue, or at least a man who has a certain amount of money. Who are the richest men in town?"

She stared at him. "First there's Godfrey Hamilton. But he's been in town too long to be the killer. I told you he owned the bank, but he's a partner in the bank with another man, James Leslie. Leslie has a lot of money, too. Then there is one lawyer, Archibald Willingham. He's probably as rich as anyone in town, but he lives in a small house and chops his own wood. Two more merchants in town have plenty of money, but they both have been here for twenty years or more."

"So, banker, lawyer, merchant, how about doctors? Doctors sometimes are rich."

"Only one sawbones in town. Doc Smith, you've met him. He rents a buggy when he needs one, lives in back of his office downtown, wears one suit year round. Not a lot of cash there, I'm afraid."

"So the banker and the lawyer. How long have they been in town?"

"I don't know," Jennifer said. "But I can find out in about ten minutes."

"You do that, and I'll have another cup of coffee and a piece of that cherry pie I spotted over there. Run along now and find out about those two men."

"You save me a piece of that pie."

He waved her out of the little café.

It was closer to twenty minutes before the Pueblo girl came rushing back to the table where Longarm sat. His pie was gone, but a second piece sat at her place. She slid into the chair and took a bite; then, when her mouth was empty, she grinned.

"We might have a clue. The lawyer, Archibald Willingham, showed up in town about five years ago with a pocketful of money. He bought out the law practice of an old gent who had most of the best clients in the county tied up. The old gent moved to Chicago.

"Since then Willingham has had his way with the law work in town and in several other small towns around here. He's a power in town. Got his man elected to the state legislature in the last election."

"Where did he come from? Where did he get his money?"

"Couldn't find that out. Nobody seems to know either answer."

"So he could have embezzled the fifty thousand dollars in Denver, read for some law, and opened up his practice here."

"Then killed Wally when he came nosing around."

"Coulda don't mean he done it. I need proof."

"The clues help a little. Willingham never goes to church, and he's been called a rattlesnake for his legal dealings more than once. He sure read some books for his law work, and he's a resident of Taos. That's most of the second series of clues."

Longarm thought about the last clues. "A small black case could be his briefcase. He uses a buggy and lives in a house, but the cough syrup, the grave marker, and the thermometer don't tie in at all."

Jennifer had finished the pie.

Longarm stood. "Let's go back out to the village and see how the old men are doing with the gab session."

"That's not a nice way to talk about our chief and the elders of the great Pueblo tribe."

"Just funnin' you. Maybe you can talk to some of the women and find out what's going on out there."

"How did you know? The women can get close and usually know how a question is coming out before the men do."

It took them twenty minutes to walk back to the pueblo buildings.

On the way Jennifer looked at Longarm curiously. "You don't think that Archibald Willingham could be the man who killed my Wally?"

"Didn't say that attal. We've got two or three kettles of fish a-cooking here, and you can't tend to one and forget the others. We got to watch all three pots at the same time, and right now I got me a feeling that this one kettle might just be about done enough so we can get it off the fire. Then we just have two kettles to watch."

"And Willingham might be one of the kettles?"

"Ayuh."

"Oh. Yes, I see. You stay out here in the shade somewhere, and I'll go inside and see if I can find the ones who know what's going on in the *kiva*." She turned and hurried away, and Longarm enjoyed the smooth, sleek way her hips worked under the town dress she wore today.

Longarm walked down to the stream and threw rocks into the water. He found a shady spot, leaned against a young ponderosa, and closed his eyes. Good time to catch up on some shut-eye.

An hour later he felt something tickle his nose. He made a slow paw at it, to scare away a fly or mosquito. It tickled him again; only this time his hand darted out, caught Jennifer Walking Dove's slender wrist, and pulled her onto his lap.

"You got to be a damn lot more Indian than that to sneak up on me," Longarm said.

Jennifer pouted. "You heard me coming?"

"About the time you stepped down from the ladder at the pueblo. What do the old women say?"

"Nothing is decided yet. The council likes the idea of the plows and the tools. They argue about the beef and raising cattle and the doctor."

"We'll give them two more hours."

She smiled. "We could find a secluded place and get out of some of our clothes and be much cooler."

"But not for long. Our bodies would heat up quickly. Best we wait a mite on that sort of slap and tickle." He moved her off his lap, and she sat beside him near the water.

"What happened back there in 1689 or whenever that the Pueblos kicked the Spaniards out of the whole territory?"

"It was 1680. We Pueblos have no written history, but the church in Santa Fe had several documents on it including a diary of a priest. He said it was a violent and cruel time. The church was pushing harder and harder to Christianize all of the Pueblos. Many were executed for violating some of the church's or the Spanish ruler's edicts.

"The savage acts and the retributions and the killings of the Indians got worse and worse until the Pueblos had suffered enough. They organized. There were many more Pueblo people then than there are today. All on the same day, the Pueblos rose up and killed many of the Spanish leaders and priests and drove the rest from the churches and the offices and hunted them down.

"In a few days thousands of Spaniards—civil, military and religious—were killed. The rest fled south out of the New Mexico area. It must have been terrible if my mild-mannered people rose up with such murderous ways.

"We are not a warrior society. We plant and grow and harvest. That is our life. We have never been at war with the United States Army, did you know that? Never once has the army come to fight with us, because we do not fight with them."

Longarm considered it. Her story was much like the official versions he had read. Close enough. It must have been mighty bad for this kind of people to rise up.

He pushed up on one arm and stared at her. "You think we could still find that secluded place by the river? Like the one we were at the other day before that bushwhacker interrupted us?"

Jennifer smiled. "I think we might be able to find such a place. The young men all work in the fields. The old men talk in the *kiva*. The old women listen at the council."

She stood, and they wandered upstream, past the end of the pueblos. They found a spot, close to the chattering stream. In this natural setting, with nothing but grass and naked bodies and the singing of the stream, Longarm saw the Indian girl in a new light, with stronger demands and wilder suggestions.

They idled away two hours at the delightful private spot by the stream; then Longarm checked his pocket watch.

"My bones tell me that things are wrapping up in the *kiva*. We better get up there so you can go have a look-hear."

Chapter 10

Back at the *kiva,* the talking was not done. Jennifer Walking Dove vanished inside the complex structure of the pueblo and found the old women who knew what was going on. She came back fifteen minutes later and pointed down the trail toward town.

"The old grandmothers say that the talking is maybe half over. The council has agreed to accept the white man's plows and his tools and his barrels. They are divided about the beef. They say, Why should they raise beef as they do corn, when the buffalo still roam the lower valleys and broad plains?"

"The buffalo are gone," Longarm snorted. "Everyone knows there haven't been any real herds for ten years."

She looked up at him and tears brightened her black eyes. "We all know that, but some of the old grandfathers will not accept it. They say that the buffalo will return. It has happened before when the buffalo didn't come to the low valleys. Then after five years they came back. Several of the old grandfathers believe they will come back."

"They're gone for good, Jennifer. They were slaughtered by the millions for their hides, fifteen years ago. There are no buffs to come back."

She wiped the tears away and caught his hand. "I know. Most of the old men know. But they want to believe." She sniffled and wiped at her eyes again. "The night of the long talk will not end until morning. We might as well work on those damn clues again."

"Morning? What's your guess on the outcome?"

"The old men have accepted the tools and barrels; they will finally approve the beef for slaughter and your starter herd. They will turn down the white man's doctor coming to the Pueblo."

"Four out of five ain't bad. Will that be enough for them to spare the life of Hamilton?"

"Grandfather wants it that way; he will convince them, but not until morning. That's what the old women say."

As they walked back to the village, Jennifer brought up the lawyer again.

"What about Archibald Willingham? You think he's the one who killed Wally and stole all the money?"

"Could be. Where's his office? Let's mosey right down there and talk with the gent."

"Just like that?"

"Why not? Like to get a gander at a man, kind of size him up. Helps more than you know."

Archibald Willingham had a ground-level legal office next to the bank in the most respectable part of town. Gold-leaf lettering on the door announced that Archibald Willingham, Attorney At Law, was ensconced within.

Longarm caught the knob, rattled it once, then pushed the heavy oak door inward slowly, allowing anyone inside to be aware of the entry.

When he had opened the door fully, he found a plush office. It had fancy oak furniture, a thick carpet on the floor, silk curtains of a muted style on the front window, and a desk almost as big as a bed. Behind it sat a man who was common enough to be anyone. He was Mr. Average.

"Mr. Willingham?" Longarm asked.

The man stood. He was five-eight, with thinning gray hair, maybe fifty years old, and wore steel-rimmed spectacles over his pale blue eyes. A slight twitch vibrated just over his right eye. Slowly he nodded.

"Yes, Marshal Long, I'm Willingham. How is your search going for the wanted man?"

"You know about my job here?" Longarm asked.

"Of course, I'm an officer of the court. I'm also hoping

you catch whoever murdered Wally Johnson so I can defend him."

"For free, of course, Mr. Willingham. It doesn't look as if you need the money."

"Looks can be deceiving." He turned toward Jennifer. "Miss Walking Dove. So good of the schoolmistress to come call on me. I see you've been our marshal's guide around Taos."

"I'm trying to help him find out who killed Wally."

"I'm sure. Now, Marshal Long, how can I be of assistance to you?"

"I'm betting that you have your eyes and ears out in this town. Have you heard anything about who the culprit might be who did in Wallace Johnson?"

"You're correct, Marshal Long. I have asked some of my people to see what they could discover, but unfortunately, they have come up with a total blank sheet of paper."

"Not even a pinch of snuff to sneeze at?"

"Not that much."

"Well, we thank you for your help. If you get any ideas about a suspect, you let me know. I'm at the hotel or just leave a message with the sheriff."

Willingham nodded, and Longarm and Jennifer walked out of the office into the noisy street. A teamster yelled at his mules. Somebody had backed a buggy into a wagon, and the two owners were screeching at each other.

A dozen feet down from the front window of the lawyer's office, Jennifer pulled Longarm to a stop and faced him. "So what do you think about Willingham? Did he kill Wally?"

"Not himself. He wouldn't get his town pants dripped with blood. He's not a knife man, not enough backbone. If he ever kills a man, which I doubt, he'll use a rifle or a handgun. Much less personal. He could have hired someone. We need more information."

Jennifer faced back toward the lawyer's office. She looked past Longarm and frowned. "Don't turn around, but your lawyer friend has just left his office in a great hurry. He turned the other way and didn't see us."

Longarm spun around, and they walked after the lawyer. He didn't look behind. He marched down the boardwalk, taking in stride the different heights of wooden planking built from store to street. When he came to the Gunplay Saloon and Gambling

Hall, he turned in the door and vanished.

"Stay here," Longarm said and slid in the same door a few seconds later, hoping the lawyer wasn't standing just inside the dark saloon.

Lawyer Willingham braced himself against the bar and had just downed a shot of whiskey. He put the glass carefully on the polished mahogany and strode through the saloon to the stairway. He took the steps three at a time with his short legs, and at the top he turned in at the first door that could be seen from below.

Longarm ambled over to the bar, ordered a needled beer from the apron, and stood there sipping the brew. At least it was cold here. They had a good icehouse just outside of town, a community ice house. They drained water from the Rio Grande into a pond at the start of winter and let it freeze two feet thick. Then they sawed the ice into one-hundred-pound chunks, dragged them from the pond, and hauled them to the icehouse.

The floor of most icehouses was coated with straw or hay; then the ice was put down with air spaces between the blocks so they wouldn't freeze together. The blocks were laid out in long rows with inches of space between. Then another layer of straw or grass went over that ice, and more ice blocks were stacked in the opposite direction on top of the first layer. This went on until the ice came to the roof of the twelve-foot cover.

Such a barn would keep ice through most of the summer. It wasn't much good for eating, but it sure kept the beer cold.

Longarm let the barkeep go past him twice, then on the third run held up his hand. The counterman stopped.

"Yeah?"

"You got girls? Don't see none on the floor."

"We got a few. Special. You got to go up and talk with Miss Dorothy."

"That door at the head of the stairs?"

"You betcha."

"Somebody there now."

"Yeah, but he's just regular business, not pussy business. You go up anytime you want."

"Finish my beer."

The conference between Miss Dorothy and lawyer Willingham took only a few more minutes. The counselor came marching back down the stairs and hurried out of the saloon, apparently not seeing anyone there. Longarm had turned his back to the fast-paced lawyer as he strode past.

He decided that Willingham's visit to this local madam was interesting but certainly not illegal, or illicit, or even ill-timed. He could find nothing to connect it in any way with the Johnson killing.

He strolled outside to find Jennifer tapping her booted foot on the dirt street.

"Been waiting for you. He'll get away." She grabbed Longarm's elbow and hurried him down the street. "When he came out of the saloon, he went to the Phillips Gunshop next door, then out of there and hightailed it straight to the Hamilton General Store."

Longarm slowed her down. "Maybe he picked up the derringer he had repaired, realized he was out of ammunition, and went over to the store to get some."

She frowned. "But I thought he killed Wally?"

"We don't have any proof. There might be three or four men in town who fit those clues we have."

"I still think he did it. I don't like the way he stares at me. What happened in the saloon?"

Longarm told her and she scowled. "That's where he set up the meetings with the men he hired to kill Wally. They could come up the back stairs and no one would see them. He could pay them off there, and only them and Miss Dorothy would know about it."

"Fine. Let's ask the lawyer man if he killed Wally. Here he comes out of the general store."

Jennifer frowned at him, her arms akimbo. "You mean just ask him if he killed Wally?"

"Why not? Maybe he has an alibi for the time of the killing."

"You ask him," she said. "I don't dare. He's on the school board."

Longarm grinned and took half a dozen strides toward the lawyer as he approached.

"Oh, Mr. Willingham. Could I have a word with you?"

"Marshal Long, of course. In my office or here in the street?"

"This will do and won't take but a couple of minutes. We've put a profile together of the man who probably killed Wally Johnson. He must be a rich man; he must have come to town about five years ago. He must not be a church member or attender, and he must have something of a reputation as a man who strikes hard and fast when a good chance arises.

"From what I can find out, you fit all of these requirements."

The lawyer's poker face showed no giveaway emotion. He nodded. "Quite a profile. How did you come up with it?"

"The dead man gave some clues to his friend, who gave them to me. I think he suspected he might be killed. So, Mr. Willingham. Where were you that night that young Mr. Johnson met his maker?"

Willingham smiled. "Good thing I know. That was the regular meeting of the Taos School Board. We met from about seven until well after eleven. Then by the time Jim and I got the women members all safely escorted home, we stopped in at a saloon for a drink. I sat in on a poker game and never got out of it until well after three A.M. I can give you the names of at least a dozen folks who watched the poker game or were in it.

"Of course the entire school board will vouch for my presence during the whole meeting. Afraid I have what I'd call an iron-reinforced alibi, Marshal Long."

"Don't be afraid at all, Mr. Willingham. You fit the profile, so you became a suspect. Hope you don't mind. Oh, by the way, how did it feel to have just a touch of the wrong side of the law bearing down at you there just now?"

The lawyer brought his heavy brows down to hood his eyes. "Felt damn peculiar, I can say that. Must be how most of the folks feel when I question them on the witness stand. Not a place I'd want to be. No, sir. I like the right side of the law."

"Thanks for your trouble."

Longarm touched his hat brim and the two parted. He walked back to Jennifer, who had stood where she could hear most of the conversation.

"You weren't terribly hard on him."

"True, no need. He's got too good an alibi. You usually can't bribe twelve men watching a poker game."

99

"He still could have hired somebody to do the killing and made sure he had that good alibi."

Longarm nodded. "Coulda, but he didn't. Just don't feel right. We got no facts. Get us some evidence, woman, something we can prove in court."

"Wish I had some. I'll watch him."

"Could be a long watch."

"So what else do we do now, just nothing?"

"Pondering that myself. I'm fed up to Texas with those clues of yours. Let's go smell hunting."

She looked at him with a puzzled frown.

"Let's go sniffing around and see if we can find that same smell I got when I had a whiff of the ambusher who could be the killer and embezzler."

"Oh. Fine." She furrowed her brow. "Just how did you describe it again?"

"Kind of a metallic smell—no, not that exactly. A little bit like the smell of coal oil, but not so strong or sharp. Softer, intense." Longarm threw up his hands and paced around in a circle. "Dammit, I don't know how to describe it, but I sure as old Fanny's underwear will know it when I smell it again."

Jennifer took a long breath and held it, shifting her eyes from side to side, then let out the pent-up air and giggled. "That was just practice. I think I'm ready for the real thing now."

He caught her elbow and propelled her down the street.

"First the Hardware store. It wasn't gun oil, no kind of oil, exactly. But . . ."

" . . . you'll know the smell when you sniff it," Jennifer continued for him. "Let's give it a try."

The hardware didn't prove productive. They worked through stacks of shovels and buckets and harness and horse collars, but nothing had the right twang.

The next spot they stopped was a café, but they walked out at once. The food smells killed everything else.

"Soap, could it have been some fancy soap? I've seen ladies' bars of soap with perfume in them."

"No, not perfume. This smell never would be confused with a perfume, not that delicate. More forceful, more demanding."

"Longarm, you've been behind a horse when it peed. That strong a smell?"

Longarm laughed. "No, not quite that strong, but that's something of the general idea. Sharp and strong, but not urine strong."

They worked through half the stores in Taos where they fancied there might be some kind of smells, but at each one they stared at each other and shook their heads.

By the time they had supper, it was getting dark.

"Another whole day shot to hell in a hand basket and good for nothing," Longarm growled as they walked along the street afterward. "Don't seem like we're getting anywhere."

"Maybe we should take the rest of the night off and rest and relax out at my house."

"Rest?"

"Well, we'd probably get in a little rest sometime before morning."

"Must be something we should do."

"We could have the doctor look at your wound."

"It's fine. He'd just want to change the dressing. That's when it hurts."

"We can't simply stand here on the street for the rest of the night."

"Let's check to see what our favorite lawyer is up to. He closed up his office and is heading across the street," Longarm said. They crossed behind him and watched. Archibald Willingham dropped off some papers at the sheriff's office and a moment later came out and walked directly to the Gunplay Saloon and Gambling Hall.

Longarm looked at the small Indian girl.

"Might be productive. You get your little bottom on home, and I'll check him out here and meet you there later. Go now, before it gets dark. I'll see you when this is over. He might get into a long poker game again, or something more productive for us. Now scat."

She glared at him for a moment with a wounded look, then softened. "Just so you show up in my bed tonight. I'll leave the kitchen light on for you." She turned and walked away, then looked over her shoulder and smiled.

Longarm hurried into the saloon and found the lawyer lifting a shot glass at the bar. He downed the whiskey in one gulp and set the glass carefully on the bar, then backed away and headed for a poker game that had one open chair.

So much for an up-close watch. Longarm knew he'd have to do it the hard way. The deputy U.S. marshal grabbed a bottle of needled beer and found a chair at an empty table where he could see the game and the side of the lawyer's face. Looked like he was in the game for a long haul. At first glance he appeared to be a man who needed a winning hand.

Longarm settled in. He called for a deck of cards for some solitaire and was told they didn't give out cards for free, so he bought a pack for a dime. He was halfway through the first game when two men came in the saloon's back door. Both looked more like saddle tramps than anything else. They had week-old beards, dirty clothes, and six-guns tied low.

Willingham looked up at them and nodded, and they took a table and got cold beers. Five minutes later Willingham said he had to go to the outhouse and tipped his chair up to save his place. He went outside, and the two scruffy men followed him a few steps later.

Longarm ambled that way and slipped through the back door, opening it in what he hoped would be a quiet way.

A lantern burned over the back door of the saloon to help the men find the outhouse and get back inside. It cast a pale glow of light right over the outside of the back door. The three men looked up as the hinges squeaked when Longarm stepped out the door.

"I'll be damned," one of the men snarled. "If it ain't that murdering bastard, Marshal Longarm."

Even in the faint light of the lantern at twenty feet, Deputy United States Marshal Longarm saw the man's right hand dig for his six-gun. Longarm didn't have to think what to do. His right hand whipped across his waist in the start of the classic cross draw.

102

Chapter 11

Longarm knew instinctively that the other man had started his draw first. As he dug for his weapon, he dropped to one knee; he swung his six-gun around as he cocked the hammer and aimed, all in the time it takes a hummingbird to flutter its wings.

Two shots came almost at the same time. The scruffy gunman had been confused by Longarm's sudden knee drop, and as he adjusted his quick sighting, he'd pulled it to the right, off target.

Longarm's round went directly through the gunman's heart, slamming him backward into the dust of the alley.

Longarm stood smoothly, his muzzle still aimed at the second rider, who hadn't drawn.

"That's it," Longarm barked. "Don't be dumb-assed and try to get out a hogleg. Who was he?"

Lawyer Willingham cleared his throat. "This gentleman who now I fear is deceased was in my employ. He and his friend here have been tracking a man I want to see brought to justice for stealing funds from his employer, the Taos State Bank.

"The man in the dust was known to me as Wild Bill Quigley, although I'm not sure that was his rightful name." The lawyer turned to the second man. "Fred, was that this man's correct name?"

The other man still stared at the body of his late friend. He shook his head, then looked up at the lawyer.

"What was that, Mr. Willingham?"

The lawyer repeated the question.

"Well, Wild Bill used several names. I don't know all of them. One was William Quantrell, another one was Wallace Quail. Then once I heard him go by the name of Win Quill. He always kept his initials the same."

"Did you say Win Quill?" Longarm asked. He let the hammer down easy on an empty round in the chamber of his gun and slid the weapon back to leather.

"Yes, sir," Fred said.

"Win Quill, was he from Arizona?"

"Mostly. Said he'd done a year in the Territorial, but we never got down to cases."

Longarm nodded. "Yeah, I remember the man now. Out of Phoenix. I was down there chasing a bank robber from Denver, and he'd teamed up with somebody named Quill. Not the kind of name you forget.

"In the shoot-out at the end of it, the other guy got gunned down by the sheriff and six deputies and me. Quill here kept his head down and threw out his gun. He lived and got off with one year in the Arizona Territorial. He was lucky."

"Not too damn lucky tonight," Willingham said. "Don't either of you move. I'll go get the sheriff, and we'll get this little matter taken care of quickly." He stared at Fred. "Then I'll expect a complete report on your progress in finding that man."

It was an hour later before the sheriff was satisfied. The undertaker came with an oversized wheelbarrow and carted the body away for its final rest.

Longarm had signed a paper agreeing to the testimony of the two witnesses. Each said that Quill had identified the deputy marshal by name, then drawn first without warning.

Lawyer Willingham nodded at Longarm as they went back into the saloon. "So, am I still a suspect? You figured to follow me awhile, and when I went out with those two mangy men, you figured you'd found Johnson's killers."

"Could have worked out that way. Any more ideas about what rich man in town killed Johnson, or had him killed?"

"Rich man. Not a lot of those around. Depends on what you mean by rich. But generally I'd say you have about ten suspects. I wish you luck. If there's a trial here in town for the murder, I still want to defend. The murder trial would take precedence in this county over any charges in Denver. Besides, we would have him in custody. First jurisdiction."

Longarm smiled. "Let's catch the killer first; then you lawyers can do your talking. That's out of my hands."

They parted, and Longarm checked his pocket watch. It was slightly after nine o'clock. He'd stop by at the Broadmoor Hotel and pick up his carpetbag and leather case and haul them out to the schoolmarm's place. If he was going to stay there, he needed the rest of his clothes.

He had just entered the lobby of the hotel when the clerk motioned to him. He walked over.

"Mr. Long. One telegram for you, brought in by mail from Santa Fe, and one more message." He handed the two sealed envelopes to Longarm, who thanked him, took his key, and walked up the stairs toward his room. He had just put his key in the door when he heard a weapon cock behind him. The sound was so close he figured he had half a chance by lunging backward. He waited.

"So?" the lawman asked.

"So, I'd say you're not being careful, Mr. Deputy U.S. Marshal Custis Long."

"Natasha," he said. He knew who it was as soon as he heard the husky voice.

He turned slowly and saw her slide a small revolver into her reticule. She was dressed more conservatively this time.

"I have a message for you. I tried to find you last night and the night before. You must be screwing the schoolmarm. Is that Indian pussy good?"

Longarm chuckled. "Natasha, you say the naughtiest things. Let's go inside and talk. Why did you try to find me last night?"

"To give you a message from Mr. Hamilton. He's worried about this matter of the dead Indian. He says he will make it well worth your time if you can help him avoid total financial ruin or his capture by the Indians."

"Natasha, you know I'm a U.S. lawman. We can't take gifts, gratuities, or bribes. But the law doesn't say anything about inviting a pretty girl into my hotel room." He unlocked the door and pushed it open hard. He looked inside from his usual position flat against the wall at the side of the door.

No shotgun blast came, and the door hit the wall, so no one was hiding behind it. He took a better look with the help of the lamp glowing in the hall. No one inside.

He stepped in, lit a lamp on the dresser, and ushered the tall lady inside.

Now in the room, he saw her in the better light. He was still surprised that she was so tall, at least five-eight. Her long brown hair cuddled around her shoulders, gleaming and bouncing in its thick and glorious way. Her widely set eyes watched him now, and her cupid mouth pouted.

"You had forgotten Natasha. Maybe you don't like Natasha anymore."

He stepped to her, caught her in his arms, and burned a hot kiss all the way through her lips until they opened and his tongue darted inside, stabbing again and again at her mouth until she whimpered.

He let her go, and she leaned her head back, eyes closed, and purred. "Yes, yes. That's what I like about a good man. He knows how to make a woman like it."

He let go of her, went to the door, and locked it, leaving the key in the hole but turned halfway so it couldn't be pushed out by another key. Then he jammed the straight-backed chair under the doorknob.

"Usual precautions," Natasha said. "I like that. But whatever can the two of us do in a hotel room all by ourselves and locked in this way?"

"We'll just have to figure out something," Longarm said. "Before you asked me for one of my wild fantasies. How about one of your wildest sexual fantasies?"

She kissed his eyes and then his lips, softly, gently, so he barely felt it. Lightning struck again, and he was jolted by the delicate touch and its amazing power.

"Fantasy . . . I've done everything several times. Why don't we just enjoy ourselves, as long as it doesn't hurt either one of us."

He undressed her slowly, kissing away each item. Under her dress she wore a corset, the kind that covered her breasts as well. He struggled with the whalebone contraption until she took pity on him and undid it herself.

"Garter belts, designed not to hold up silk stockings, but to get a man's prick up the minute he spots them. Do they really hold up the hose?"

She laughed and kissed him and took off his shirt.

When they both were naked, she turned him over on his stomach and without a word began to massage his feet. She worked his ankles, then up the back and sides of his legs, and by the time she turned him over to work on the tops of his legs, his full and eager erection pulsated like a diesel engine.

"Woman, what are you doing to me?"

"Getting you relaxed so we can make perfect, unmatched love." She kissed his penis from head to roots, then ignored it, rolled him over, and worked on his sides and his back. When she came to his neck, he felt as if his body were a bowl full of chocolate pudding, without a single bone.

She rolled him over on his back, caught his erection, and in one swift motion, dropped down on him, impaling her vagina with his throbbing cock.

"Oh, damn," Longarm bellowed, then tried to kiss her. "I'm in heaven. Just don't wake me up. What a hell of a great dream."

"No dream, lover. Just skill and understanding of the male body and how you cockhound men always think. You first or me?"

Longarm prided himself on being able to control the order of climaxing, almost always waiting for the lady to take her pleasure first. But this time he had no control. She squeezed him with her internal muscles, and in the time it took him to make three hard, fast plunges into her, he unloaded his whole wad. Then he pounded upward a dozen times more to be sure he had deposited all of his wealth in her vault.

"Oh, damn!" he gasped.

He opened his eyes five minutes later, when his breathing had returned to normal and he could talk again.

"How did you do that?"

"What?"

"Make it so damn marvelous for me?"

"I told you. I know how men are hinged together, where the soft spots are, what nerve endings to push, and where to make your whole body turn into one big marshmallow."

"You sure as hell do. What about your turn?"

She smiled at him and touched his hair, smoothing it back. "You were out of it while I enjoyed myself. Four climaxes if I remember right. You must have been nearly unconscious. I even howled like a mountain wolf."

She pulled away from him and lay next to his long, muscled body.

"Did you really work for your government, in Europe?"

"Of course. I was one of four specialists. Unfortunately my government lasted only two years, and then several of us had to leave the country rather quickly."

"The new regime didn't like some of the ... work ... that you did for the old regime?"

Natasha smiled. "Something like that. But now I am in America and I am out of my old line of work."

"What's your new line of employment?"

"The proper ladies of Taos call me a whore. I tell them that I am no more of a whore than those properly married females. They give up sex for security. I give up sex for security. What's the difference? My security isn't until death do us part."

She reached over and began to work on his limp prick. He caught her hand and stopped her.

"So you think all women are whores?"

"No, I think there are no whores. All women fuck men for some financial reason. Might be family and home and fidelity for as long as they both shall live. Other women fuck men for two dollars a throw down in the saloons and bawdy houses. What's the difference?"

"And then some women fuck the richest man in town and get kept in his big house and bought presents and dresses and fine things to eat," Longarm said.

"Yes. True. When he tells me to deliver a message to Mr. Deputy United States Marshal Custis Long, I do it. If I stay around to get poked a few times, he doesn't care."

"So you think all women at heart are fucking for security. What about men?"

"You guys. Easy. All men at heart at the best are rampaging range bulls, trying to get their cocks in as many of us cows as possible. At the worst, men are rapists."

Longarm reached over and kissed her. "You like to speak your mind, don't you, Natasha?"

"In my country that was not a good idea. Now, here in America, I can speak my mind, my thoughts. I might be wrong, but I can be wrong loud and in the middle of town and no one will arrest me."

"True. It's called freedom. We fought to get it, we'll fight to keep it. Now, one more question. Tell me about your work in Europe. Tell me about one case you worked on for your government."

"No, absolutely not."

He kissed her and caressed her breasts, and when his lips came away from hers, she whimpered.

"You are not supposed to be able to do that to me, Custis Long. The goody-goody women call me the town whore with no feelings."

He kissed her again, and this time his hand slid between her thighs and massaged the soft, damp place between her legs. She moaned in anticipation.

"Now, delightful lover, tell me about killing someone in Europe."

"Oh damn you. I promised I'd never tell anyone." She shrugged and nibbled on his fingers. "Just this once. He was the director of our secret police. He was not a nice man. The president of our country decided the director was planning on killing him and taking over power.

"Two days before the plot was to explode with the president in a flaming carriage, I called on the director of secret police with a message from the president. Because I was a woman, they allowed me in with no guards present. That was in case the director wanted to utilize the soft bed he had through a connecting door, in his private quarters.

"The message was not that important. A pat on the back for a job well done. A guarantee that he would be director of the secret police for as long as the president ruled. It pleased the director, and he invited me to his private rooms for a snack of imported caviar and British crackers with wine and cheese.

"We snacked and drank the wine; then he asked me to take off my clothes. He said he had to check for any hidden weapons. He checked me everywhere but one body cavity. Then he threw me to his bed and tried to rape me, but I helped him so much it frustrated him. After the third time he was so exhausted that he could barely move.

"In his small-death, I pulled the two-inch capsule from my body cavity, opened it, extended an inch-long blade, and before he knew what was happening, I cut both of the carotid arteries in his neck. I sat there fascinated by the spurting of the blood with each heartbeat. His blood flew all the way to the twelve-foot ceiling!

"The director was dead within two minutes. I dressed, slipped out the door, flirted with the guards outside, then walked out of the secret police headquarters and back to the presidential palace.

"The next morning the secret police announced that the director had suffered a massive heart attack during the night. A team of top doctors in our capitol had worked over him for six hours, but they couldn't save this hero of the people.

"Two months later, our president was overthrown by a clique of army generals, and about forty of us were permitted to leave the country but with no more than fifty dollars' worth of money and valuables.

"I did a job no man could have done. In that place, no man was ever alone with the director of the secret police. Not even when the man was in his command. He tried so hard to live, but it took a woman to undo him."

"That could never happen in our country," Longarm said. "In our government we have a series of checks and balances between the three sections of government—the executive, the legislative, and the judicial."

Natasha nodded and rolled over on top of him. "Hey, big deputy U.S. marshal. You going to lay there talking all night? Don't you think a woman likes a man who's not shot to hell for at least four days after one climax? Get it up and let's get back to the fun part. You're next for the fantasy."

Longarm couldn't remember when they at last went to sleep. It wasn't dawn, but he had seen some streaks of light in the east. Just as well he didn't know. Some folks said a body needed eight hours of sleep to function. Hell, if that was true, he wasn't functioning most of the time.

Longarm rolled out of bed at 6:30 A.M. Natasha lay sleeping with the light blanket over her to ward off the seven-thousand-foot chill of the night air.

He whipped it back in one motion, but she never moved. Her eyes fluttered but didn't open.

"Longarm, put that back or I'll get out my scalpel and make that longarm of yours into a short arm."

The deputy U.S. marshal roared with laughter, spread the covers back carefully, and then lay on top of them, on top of her, and kissed her eyes open.

"Better?"

"Delightfully better. Now I should get up, too. Godfrey likes to see me around the house when he rises about nine, even though he's in no condition to use my body."

She dressed as he shaved in the cold water from the pitcher. When he'd wiped the shaving soap off his face, she kissed his cheek, touched his shoulder, and smiled.

"I'll be back. Any message for Godfrey?"

"Yes. Tell him the negotiations should have been finished last night in the *kiva*. I expect that he will be spared being toasted over a Pueblo Indian fire. But it will cost him a good deal in money and material. I'll see him when I'm sure of the outcome."

She touched his shoulder again, then stepped out the door and hurried down the hall.

Today he should know about the Pueblo council's decision. He dressed and hurried over to the schoolmarm's house. The shaving and the upper-body sponge bath he had given himself had removed all of Natasha's scent from him.

The lamp still burned in the kitchen but was almost out of coal oil. He blew it out and tiptoed toward the bedroom. A shotgun barrel pushed out of the partly open door.

"One more step and you get double-aught buckshot right through your middle."

"Jennifer, it's me, Custis. Put that thing down."

She didn't put it down. Rather she opened the door and kept the gun leveled at him. Jennifer Walking Dove wore only what she'd been born in. Her face was frozen into a mask of anger. "Aren't you a little late?"

"I got held up. A guy tried to kill me. I had to shoot him, and then I had to do a report for the sheriff. Turned out that lawyer friend of yours was meeting with two saddle bums. They were working for him on another case."

"That took all night?"

111

"I'll tell you about it over breakfast. I'm buying. Get dressed and we'll go eat and then out to the pueblos and find out what your grandfather decided."

Slowly she nodded. "Yes, you're right. Don't worry about the shotgun. It has never been loaded. Purely defensive." She looked at him again and frowned, started to say something but didn't.

It was after eight before they arrived at the pueblos. Longarm didn't think that he'd ever seen so many of the Indians in and around the area. Walking Dove hurried into a ground level apartment, and Longarm threw stones in the creek.

When he looked up again, there were about two hundred Pueblo Indians, some dressed in their finest, gathering at the largest of the structures.

Jennifer Walking Dove hurried up to him. She wore a big grin. "I guessed right. Yes to all but the sawbones. We're having a march to the burial mounds to make the agreement with the white chiefs."

Longarm held up both hands. "First let me go get Godfrey Hamilton and the city council and a batch of the white eyes."

She caught his upraised hand and held it. "They have already been notified to be at the river at nine o'clock. That's when we'll agree to the terms of the repayment for the death of Red Feather."

Chapter 12

Longarm's Waterbury showed it was a half hour until the big announcement at the river.

"We've got to get to Hamilton and tell him what it's going to cost him so he isn't surprised," Longarm said.

As they hurried to the rich man's main office near the bank, Longarm remembered the two messages he'd received the night before from the room clerk. One was a telegram mailed in from Santa Fe. Probably from Chief Marshal Billy Vail in Denver. It would have to wait until he got back to his hotel room. He had no idea what the other message might be.

They got to Godfrey Hamilton's office twenty minutes before the meeting at the river. Hamilton was in and glowering.

"I hear the Injuns got themselves some ideas what I should do to keep my scalp," Hamilton said.

Longarm stared at him. "Mr. Hamilton, you have three choices. You can pay up what the Indians demand, you can run out of town and lose everything that you own here, or you can try to stay and keep your goods and wind up getting toasted head-down over a Pueblo camp fire. The choice is up to you. I'd strongly suggest you pay up for your dirty deed. If you go along with the Indian demands, I'll dismiss that federal attempted murder charge against your son."

Hamilton stalked to the window and came back, his face not quite so angry. "When you put it that way, I guess I must at least listen to what the savages have to say."

"You were the savage, Mr. Hamilton, when you rode down Red Feather with your horse," Jennifer Walking Dove snapped.

He looked at her, and the last of his anger evaporated. He slumped in his desk chair, his head down. "All right, what will they demand?"

Longarm told him exactly what the Indians had agreed to ask for. When he finished, the businessman had written it all down. He stared at the list and made some quick calculations. His face turned red and he jumped up.

"You know how much money that will cost?"

"Maybe three thousand dollars, give or take a brood cow or two," Longarm said. "A damn sight cheaper than spending ten years in the territorial prison, or getting roasted over a hot camp fire. Face it, Hamilton. You made a fool of yourself, and you killed another human being. Now you pay for it."

"What if I don't?"

"I have other ways, Hamilton. First your son goes on trial. Then there's a new federal law that applies here. I can arrest anyone who interferes with or causes great bodily harm or financial loss to any ward of the United States Government. Hamilton, you're smart enough to know that this law was passed especially to protect the Indian tribes from unscrupulous white men. It applies here. You can get five years in a federal penitentiary for killing Red Feather. The trial would be short, the sentence quick. Is that what you want?"

"You wouldn't do that. He was just an Indian!"

"And you are *just a white man!*" Jennifer screeched at him.

"He was a human being," Longarm went on. "You people are going to have to learn to live with the Indians. They are here to stay. They become more able to live with the white men all the time."

Longarm watched the businessman lose his anger again. He bowed his head on the desk and beat one fist on the hard wood. "So now, Hamilton, which of the three paths are you going to follow?"

He looked up, and they saw that he had been weeping. "Hell, you know I've only got one option. So it costs me thirty-five hundred or four thousand dollars, that's better than running away from them and from you. Hell yes, I'll buy them the goods, and deliver them, and you don't press charges against my son. Then I hope that will be the end of it."

"Your horse ranch?"

"Damn, you never give up. Yes, I'll change my plans and move the ranch far down the valley, away from the Indian mounds. No more harm will come to the old graveyard."

"We should be going to the river," Jennifer said.

They walked out of the building and found half the people of the town moving toward the river.

Jennifer Walking Dove waded across the small headwaters of the Rio Grande and met with her grandfather on the other side. She had taken a written list of what the Indians would ask for, and when she decided that enough were present on both sides of the river, she held up her hands and everyone quieted. Then Jennifer spoke.

"The council of elders of the Taos Pueblo tribe has considered the matter of the accidental death of Red Feather and, after long consideration, has come with this set of demands from the white man killer Godfrey Hamilton.

"Since the death was an accident, we don't demand the death penalty, but the following tribute must be paid."

She listed the items that had been agreed upon, and with each one there was a gasp from the white listeners. When she had finished telling about the herd of cattle and the steers for butchering, she held up her hands again to quiet the white side.

"These are the demands of the council of the Taos Pueblo tribe. How does the killer Godfrey Hamilton answer to them?"

Hamilton walked close to the river and motioned for those standing by him to move away. He then turned to the Indian side and spoke softly.

"Shout your words, Mr. Hamilton, so I can translate them to my people," Jennifer Walking Dove demanded. "Speak in short sentences and pause after each so I can translate for my people."

Hamilton's voice wavered then rose to a resounding pitch more like what he must have used as a Baptist preacher.

"I accept the demands of the Taos Pueblo council." He paused and Jennifer translated. When she said his words in her native language, a cheer went up from the Indians.

She continued to translate after each sentence.

Hamilton continued: "All goods and animals will be delivered as quickly as possible. There are two walking plows in stock and the necessary tools. They will be transported to the village this afternoon.

"The barrels will take some time, and the brood cattle and steers will have to be found in the surrounding countryside and delivered to the tribe. This should take no more than a week. I will comply fully with all that you ask."

After the last sentence had been translated, Chief Running Fox called out a question to his granddaughter. She listened, then nodded and turned to the other side of the river.

"Mr. Hamilton. My grandfather, Chief Running Fox, asks what you intend to do about the horse ranch and house you planned to put up on Indian sacred lands."

"I will change my plans and move this ranch well downstream from the sacred ground," Hamilton answered.

Jennifer translated the words to the Indians, and again there was a burst of approval from the Pueblos.

Jennifer nodded and looked at the whites.

"My grandfather says to you, It is good, it is finished. Now we will live in peace."

Jennifer spoke with her grandfather for a moment, then came across the stream, and the meeting was over. Indians and whites alike on each side of the creek turned and hurried back to their usual activities.

Walking Dove came up to Longarm and nodded.

"It is done."

"Good. Now I need to go back to the hotel. I have two messages there I want to check out. Then I suggest we talk with your grandfather about returning certain artifacts to the grave site that were stolen."

Jennifer said that was a good idea.

A few minutes later Longarm picked up the two messages from the top of the hotel-room dresser, where he had dropped them when Natasha accosted him the night before.

He ripped open the plain white envelope. Inside he found a brief note from Natasha asking for him to meet her for dinner. It was dated two days ago.

The telegram looked more important. Longarm tore it open and read it.

"Custis Long. Broadmoor Hotel. Taos, New Mexico. Please report soonest on your progress on the Johnson embezzlement case. People here are pressuring me. Send night wire as soon as possible." It was signed, Billy Vail.

Longarm sighed. He wrote out a reply, put it in an envelope with instructions to send it collect, and addressed the envelope to the telegrapher at the train depot in Santa Fe. That was the closest telegraph.

Downstairs the hotel clerk said the message would go out on the afternoon stage and should be in Santa Fe that night and sent from there almost at once. They had a twenty-four-hour telegrapher at Santa Fe.

Jennifer had waited for him in the lobby.

"Grandfather?" she asked.

He nodded. This was going to be a tougher job than he had first thought. He had brought the three-inch gold statue with him from his hotel room. How could he convince Chief Running Fox about the gold treasures that must be kept hidden?

They found the chief of the Taos Pueblo in the plaza looking in wonder at a load of spades, hoes, and rakes that had just been unloaded from a wagon. They were new, with painted handles and hard steel shanks. The old man nodded and grinned.

"We need to palaver," Longarm said to the Indian.

Chief Running Fox said something sharply to one of the men nearby, who took control of the tools. Then the chief waved Longarm with him toward one of the ladders that slanted up next to the ground-level apartments.

A few moments later they were seated on straw mats in the first-level room, and Longarm took the small gold statue from his pocket.

"Great Chief Running Fox, do you know about gold?"

"Gold?" the old Indian asked. "White man's clay. No good. Too soft."

"Is there any of this white man's clay around here deep in the mountains?"

"No. White men always search. Never find."

"None at all?"

"None."

"Did your grandfather's grandfathers ever use gold?"

"Our storytellers have many tales, but none that speak of the white man's clay. I know of its value to the white men, but the Pueblo people understand none of that."

"Chief, I was at that violated grave first that morning. I found this just inside. This gold and about twenty other pieces, all larger, were inside that tomb of one of your ancestors."

Chief Running Fox stared at Longarm, a frown building on his face. He turned to Walking Dove. She nodded.

"It is true, Grandfather."

"How can this be?"

Longarm told him his theory about the Aztecs and their extensive use of gold and how many, many years ago a large population of Aztecs from Mexico must have been in this area.

"Perhaps they made friends with your ancestors. Perhaps it is an Aztec chief who is buried there with all of his gold. I don't know. I doubt if there is any way we can discover the truth about the gold."

"Then what should we do?" the chief asked. "White men go crazy over the yellow clay."

"It's my suggestion that we tell no white men about this. If they knew, some unsavory ones would try to open the graves and hunt for more gold. All of the grave robbers but one are dead. The one in jail will hang for murder. He is being closely controlled and anything he says discounted."

"Grandfather, we think there is one more man in town who may suspect about the gold. He is the one who hired the six to dig into the tombs. We must find him."

"All of this gold, it must be returned to the grave," Chief Running Fox said. "Whoever was buried there must be in agony over the loss."

"I agree, Chief. Tonight, you are to bring one trusted warrior who is strong and two of your new shovels. We will open the tomb and replace the artifacts, then seal it up again, and no one will know about it but us. Then we must keep the secret.

"If the story ever gets out, there would be white-man raids on the tombs, and Pueblo attacks and retaliation, horrible bloodshed and a war of terrible costs to both sides. We can't permit that to happen."

"Yes, you speak truth. We will be there at the middle of the night."

"Yes, twelve o'clock by the white man's watch," Longarm said. "Just the four of us. You must send your usual burial-mound guards away out of sight for the opening of the tomb and the transfer of the gold."

The old Indian nodded, thanked Longarm for his help with the death payment from the white chief, and the lawman and Walking Dove left the first level of the pueblo and turned toward the village of Taos.

"Can we do all this in secrecy?" Jennifer asked.

"We must. And we have to track down the culprit who had the idea to raid the tomb in the first place. That could be anyone in town with a hankering for gold."

"That makes it everyone except about ten women and no men," the schoolmarm said.

Longarm massaged his jaw. "Who in a town like this would be the most interested in gold?"

"Anyone who wants to get rich."

"No, more interested than that. Who uses gold? The man who paints those names on doors in gold leaf. What if he could get his gold leaf free? Or what about the dentist? You know how many people have gold fillings in their teeth these days, and even whole new gold teeth? Right there we have two prime suspects."

Jennifer giggled. "Well, our dentist, the only one in town, is a little over eighty years old and still at work. Only he says gold is poison for the system and he won't use it for fillings. He uses something else I never figured out. But mostly he just yanks a hurting tooth out. Says that's the best way to fix it. Not a mite of gold is put in anyone's mouth here in Taos."

"Well, it was a good idea. What about the man who puts gold leaf on the doors?"

"Sorry again, Longarm. Nobody in town is that good. We don't have more than half a dozen doors with that fancy gold lettering. To get that done you have to hire a man to come out from Santa Fe. He charges you the transportation, plus the hotel bill and his meals and all of his expenses as well as a full day's work for a two-hour job. Price is high. Don't guess we have a prospect there."

Since it was almost noon by then, they settled for steak dinners at the Ponderosa Cafe. Longarm still worried over the gold problem and who had hired the grave robbers. He cut a slice off the still-sizzling steak, served on a hot iron plate, and chewed contentedly. Steak was ten times as good when it was served as soon after cooking as possible.

"Who else in town might have a business kind of use for gold?" Longarm asked. The Indian girl shook her head and her short black hair bounced.

They had almost finished their meal when Longarm looked over at Jennifer and grinned. He used his steak knife and pointed it at the woman at the next table. She was evidently one of the leading socialites of Taos, if it had any. She was dressed as if she were going to a fancy dinner or ball.

On the right front of her dress near her shoulder she wore a large gold pin that had a beautiful piece of turquoise in it.

Longarm and Jennifer looked at each other and grinned.

"A jewelry store owner," they said softly, almost in unison.

"So that gives us another tack," the lawman said. "How many jewelers in town make original pieces?"

"Only one. I tried to get some turquoise set in silver, and the two places I went sent me to the third. The other two sell a few diamonds, but mostly they repair watches and clocks."

"Who makes his own?"

"Otto Zemberling, Zemberling Jewelers, about half a block down from the bank. He has the best supply of rings and gold settings, diamonds and rubies and all the precious stones. He's said to be one of the richest men in town as well."

"Good. Be nice to wrap this up with one swoop. Any chance he could only have been in town for five years?"

"Afraid not. He was in business here when I was a small girl."

Longarm didn't hurry his meal. "No sense in letting a good steak dinner go to waste," he said. He had a second bottle of beer with the steak and all the fixings.

Nearly a half hour later, Longarm paid the check and escorted Jennifer out of the café. They walked down the street to the jewelry store. For a moment Longarm looked in the plate-glass window in front and checked the display. Lots of jewelry, a few fine watches, gold-filled, and many sample gold settings for rings and brooches.

"Worth a try," Longarm said. They went in, and when the small man behind the counter first saw the lawman, his mood and his expression changed. It wasn't a big change, but enough to set off alarm bells in the marshal's mind.

"Mr. Zemberling. I'm Deputy United States Marshal Custis Long. I'd like to talk to you about gold."

The man came to the counter, shook hands with Longarm, and smiled. But there was no truth in the smile.

"What can I do for you? Something in a gold-filled pocket watch? I have some with the finest movements."

"No, I'm more interested in gold that would be melted down, say for settings for a ring."

The jeweler looked at his own timepiece. "If you will excuse me, I have some gold melting in my back room right now. Melted gold will wait for no man. Let me tend to it. I need to check it and perhaps pour two molds, then I shall return and be able to tell you whatever you want to know about my way of creating fascinating fine art jewelry pieces for the gentleman or the lady. Please excuse. Liquid gold must be dealt with properly."

He smiled, turned, and exited through a curtain drawn across an open door that evidently led into his metallurgy workshop.

Longarm raised his brows as the man left. He looked at Jennifer.

"Sounds like a good reason to leave," Jennifer whispered.

"Could be. I'll give him two minutes."

They looked around the store. All of the gems, jewels, and fine watches were in glass-topped cases. Longarm guessed that the doors on all the cases had locks on them. Prudent.

He drummed his fingers on one of the cases, then called, "Mr. Zemberling." He waited a moment. "Mr. Zemberling, we really need to talk to you."

Another pause and Longarm whipped the Colt .44-40 from his cross-draw rig and stepped around the counter. In one swift move he swept the drape aside and stepped past it through the doorway. The back room of the jewelry shop was indeed set up for casting precious metals and making jewelry, but there was no hot gold, and no Zemberling.

Longarm darted to the door at the back of the room and flung it open. The tall, lean lawman found himself in the alley behind the jewelry store.

Jennifer ran up beside him. "Gone. Where?"

"You know where he lives?"

"Let's see. Zemberling. Yes, he has a child in school. His home isn't more than two blocks from here." She turned and ran down the alley. Longarm was soon right beside her.

"Has he been in town long?"

"For at least ten years. He couldn't be the embezzler or the killer."

"But he could have sent those men to dig into that burial mound. How much farther?"

They arrived at a cross street and turned right. That took them out of the business section. Longarm could see several houses in the block ahead.

"Up there, the fourth house from the corner," Jennifer said. "I remember it because I had to take assignments to the little girl when she was sick last year."

"You go to the front door and knock hard. Pound on the door. I'll be at the back to see if he tries to get away again."

They parted two doors down from the suspect's house and hurried to the front and back doors. Jennifer pounded on the front door, heard nothing, and pounded again.

Less than a minute later, Longarm watched the rear door open and Otto Zemberling rush out with a valise in his hand. The U.S. deputy marshal put one round from his Colt into the door beside the small man, and he dropped his valise, his face showing terror.

"What . . . what do you want? Why did you shoot at me?"

"I didn't shoot at you or you'd be dead. I need to have a quiet little talk with you. Is your family home?"

"Yes."

"Then leave that bag and we'll walk down the street. Why did you run away from us at your store?"

"You came asking about gold."

"Nothing illegal in your having gold. That's your business."

"But I thought you wanted to know about . . ."

Longarm rubbed his jaw. The man had done little wrong, even though he must have been the one who hired the grave robbers. The only trouble was the marshal would have a hard time proving that in court once a good lawyer got hold of Zemberling.

"Mr. Zemberling. I'm not asking you to admit to a thing, or to tell me anything. I want you to be certain that whatever rumors you may have heard over the years about those Pueblo chief's tombs don't have a bit of truth in them. This tribe has never had anything to do with gold. White man's clay they call it.

"Some men did dig into one of the graves. I don't know why, but they were chased off and none of the ancient artifacts in the tomb were disturbed. Who would want a four-hundred-year-old skull or a bow and arrow that had rotted in place beside the skeleton? There was absolutely nothing of any value, except maybe to a historian of some kind, in that grave."

Zemberling frowned as they walked half a block away from his house. Now he turned and looked at the lawman. "You mean you didn't come to arrest me?"

"Now, why would I do that, Mr. Zemberling?"

"Well, you are a lawman, and you asked about gold. Sometimes folks sell me old gold, and since it's in such bad condition, I have to melt it down and recast it, and I don't always pay the best price for it, and—"

"How you conduct your business is up to you, Mr. Zemberling. I have absolutely no jurisdiction in that matter. But when it comes to how whites deal with the Indians, I do have some small say-so."

Zemberling shivered and shook his shoulders as if to revitalize himself. "Well, Mr. Longarm. I have always had the best of relations with the Pueblos. Not a one of them is a customer. Yes, I do admit that I've heard a wild rumor or two about those burial mounds, but I never held any real belief in any of them. Now, since you say there's nothing of value in them, there isn't. That's about that."

"Glad you feel that way, Mr. Zemberling. Now you better get back to your store before somebody decides to help himself to some of your goods."

"Oh, damn!" Zemberling said and scurried for Main Street and his shop.

Longarm walked through a side yard to the street and found Jennifer Walking Dove waiting for him.

Chapter 13

That afternoon, Longarm rented a horse and hurried back to where he had hidden the gold artifacts in the woods, where the shoot-out with the grave robbers had taken place. He brought along a pair of strong burlap bags, put the gold figures and statues in them, and rode to town a roundabout way. He made certain no one followed him.

For the rest of the afternoon and the evening he stayed in the schoolmarm's house, guarding the gold figures. He didn't examine them; he didn't want to be able to remember them or identify them.

They spent the time worrying about who Wallace Johnson's killer, the embezzler, might be and poring over the clues, but they came up with no new ideas about his identity.

Promptly at midnight they arrived at the river across from the burial mounds. Jennifer waded across the ankle-deep stream and waited with the Pueblo Indian guards.

Longarm rode the horse with the gold downstream fifty yards and crossed over, then waited in a patch of brush.

The signal came within five minutes: the cry of the night hawk from the burial mounds, in a slightly higher pitch than usual. Jennifer. He rode forward, and she came running out to meet him.

Already an Indian man was at work digging out the side of the mound that had been violated. Chief Running Fox had pulled the guards back around the mounds, and only the four of them worked there in the faint moonlight. Longarm stepped down and helped dig with another one of the new shovels. It took them only ten minutes to penetrate the tomb.

The warrior slid inside the grave with pitch sticks and lit one, and soon Longarm was kneeling outside and passing the golden statues and figures into the Pueblo man.

Five minutes later all twenty pieces were back in place on the earthen shelves, and the warrior blew out the pitch-wood torch and climbed out of the tomb.

A half hour after the Indian came out, he and Longarm had the tomb mounded up again and sealed.

The warrior vanished into the night. Jennifer spoke quietly with her grandfather, and then she joined Longarm, and the two rode the horse back downstream before they crossed to the other side and returned the mount to the livery.

"Grandfather thanks you again for what you have done for the Pueblo people," Jennifer said as they walked toward her house.

"It should work," Longarm said. "We won't have any trouble with that man on trial. He won't say a word about that gold or the tombs."

"How can you be sure of that?"

"The sheriff has ways. That's as good as done. Now what about my embezzler? Can we finally get back to the reason I came to town in the first place?"

"Sure. I'm just as interested in finding out who killed Wally as you are."

Longarm sighed. "Sorry, I wasn't thinking. As I recall, when we talked about rich suspects, you mentioned the banker, one James Leslie. When you went out investigating, did you stop with Willingham or did you find out about Leslie, too?"

They were nearly at her back door. They usually used it, just to stop any excess idle talk. Jennifer looked up at the marshal and nodded. "You asked for both, so I got both. We talked about the lawyer first."

She unlatched the back door and walked inside the small schoolmarm's house. Longarm struck a match and found a lamp on the back porch. He lit it, and they went into the kitchen and straight to the bedroom, where he put down the lamp.

"So how long has the banker been in town?"

"A little over six years, which puts him in our suspicion range. The people I talked to said they thought he came from Chicago, or maybe San Francisco; they weren't sure."

"He's rich. Let's not worry about any of the other clues. That one should be enough for now. In the morning we start working on him."

"How?"

"I don't have the foggiest notion. Just sort of play it the way the trail leads."

Jennifer nodded, stretched, and yawned. She unbuttoned the top of her dress and turned toward Longarm.

"Hey, sexy man. Have you ever slept in the same bed with a willing woman and not made love with her?"

Longarm scowled and snorted. "Of course, lots of times."

Jennifer grinned. "Yeah, I bet. Make that a little more definite, like how many times?"

"Oh, fifty, maybe . . . well, twenty. No, more like twice that I can remember. Not the kind of a record that a grown man likes to think about."

Jennifer reached up and kissed his cheek. "Good. Tonight makes three times. I'm tired enough to go to sleep right in the middle of an orgasm, and I don't want that to happen. So just keep it soft tonight and don't tempt me. Agreed?"

Longarm bounced his head up and down. "Agreed. I could stand about six hours of undisturbed sleep. Oh, I hope you don't snore."

She threw a pillow at him.

The next morning, they had breakfast in the house and went over what they knew about James Leslie. It wasn't much. They continued their search at the post office in the Hamilton General Store.

Minerva Ihander had been postmistress in Taos for more than ten years.

"Yep, my job is to know who's here and who's moved. I keep some of it writ down just so I don't boggle my own amazing brain. Course you know all of this is confidential."

She looked at Longarm again. "I might have spoke too quick. Reckon you and me work for the same boss. You be that Deputy United States Marshal Long, I'd guess."

"That's right Mrs. Ihander. We're working on a case here and I do need your cooperation."

Minerva glowed. "Hey, no trouble. I usually don't get quite so much attention. What kind of information do you need?"

"How long has James Leslie been in town?"

"Let's see. He came in and bought the bank just at the time they put up the new building. That was six years ago come September."

"Do you know where he lived before he came here?"

"Chicago. He used to get mail from there all the time."

"Did he get any mail from or send any to Denver?"

"Yes, indeed. From the parfumed envelope I'd say she had to be a right nice catch. But somehow it didn't work out and the sweet-smelling letters stopped."

"Any family or business kind of mail from Denver?"

"Now and then. James gets a lot of mail, being a banker. More folks write him than he writes to, course."

"Is he a married man?"

"Oh, yes, brought a wife with him. Nice little thing. On the thin side for good childbearing, but then they don't have any children. Maybe that's why. A body never knows."

Longarm touched his wide-brimmed Stetson with two fingers. "We thank you, Mrs. Ihander. Oh, appreciate if you would keep this all confidential. Man may be as innocent as a newborn colt."

"Not a word. Folks hereabouts know I don't blab."

The marshal and Jennifer waved, left the store, and headed down the boardwalk.

"Sounds promising," she said.

"Indeed it does. Let's see if the sheriff is in."

Sheriff Nathan Murdock looked up in surprise. "Longarm, you coming to see me and don't have a pile of dead bodies in tow? You must be taking it easy on my constituents."

"I just shoot the out-of-towners who can't vote anyway, Sheriff. Interested in a small matter you should know about."

The sheriff provided a chair for Jennifer, but he and Longarm stood.

"I'm looking to see if you have any kind of a record on James Leslie."

"The banker?"

"The same."

"Hell no. Nothing. He ain't even shortchanged anybody that I know of. He's parson pure far as the law goes. He's never even been inside my office, let alone decorated one of my three jail cells. You thinking about him on the Johnson case?"

"Doing some speculation. He came to town about the right time. He's rich. He even sends and gets letters from Denver."

"So you've got nothing is what you're telling me. I can't help with any hard evidence, or even any speculation. He's about as straight a shooter as we got in this here town."

Longarm scowled. "Just about what I was afraid of. He's in the usual conservative mold of a banker? Doesn't drink too much, never gambles in the saloons, never tickles the whores?"

"Sums him up good," the sheriff said. "Only one thing, he ain't a church man. Figured he would be, but he told me once he just didn't cotton to that kind of thing. Used to be a Congregationalist, he said, so maybe that's why he backslid so danged far."

"Figures," Longarm said. "Thanks for not helping us much, Sheriff Murdock. We'll see what else we can find out."

Longarm was almost out the door when he turned. "Oh, has his bank ever been robbed?"

The sheriff nodded. "Truth be known he's been taken down twice. First time four years ago, when five armed men hit the place just at opening. They shot a teller in the leg, made the customers crowd into a corner, and got away with over four thousand dollars.

"Next time was about two years ago. Three men hit him just at close-up time. We never knew he'd been robbed until he managed to untie himself about midnight. The robbers took more than five thousand that time and got away clean."

Longarm rubbed his chin. "Any sign of collusion between the robbers and the bank owner?"

"Cahoots? Naw. Not a nibble. I figured there might be on that second one where nobody got hurt and all, but I dug around with all the six eyewitnesses inside the bank during the holdup, including three customers. They all said it was a slick, professional bank robbery. I let it stand."

Longarm waved, and he and Jennifer went outside.

"So what do you think about Leslie?" she asked.

"Maybe we should talk to him. Ask him for his help. If he's in this, he might slip up somewhere. I doubt if he'll run like that little jewelry maker did."

"Are you going to talk to him? Accuse him?" Jennifer asked.

"Why?"

"He's on the school board. I'd be sure to lose my job."

"Hadn't thought of accusing him. He's no lawyer. He'd probably get furious and throw me out of his office. I need some better plan with him."

"Any ideas?"

"That's supposed to be your department, Jennifer."

"No ideas." She grinned at him.

"What?" he asked noticing the strange little smile on her pretty face.

"Oh, nothing, just girl stuff."

"Like what?"

"Like last night. I really loved being cuddled up against your back knowing nothing sexy was going to happen. All I had to do was relax and go to sleep."

Longarm laughed softly. "I kind've had something of the same feelings. It was so damn ... comfortable."

They looked at each other for a minute, then walked on up the street.

She broke the silence. "I have an idea. You can go into the bank, show him your badge, and ask his help on something. Maybe a bank robber you've chased before. Has he ever seen the man? Was he one of the ones who hit his bank? Maybe something about a default on a large check issued on his bank by a customer."

Longarm stopped. "Good idea on the draft. Where's the bank?"

James Leslie was a tall and stately man. He had to be formal on all occasions, and for a brief moment Longarm wondered how formal he could be naked, panting, and straddling a sex-crazed woman.

The bank president and co-owner was six-foot-two, with a shock of jet-black hair meticulously combed. His features were subdued—soft gray eyes, a modest nose, a slightly thin mouth—giving the overall impression of a man you could trust not only with your money, but your sixteen-year-old virgin daughter as well. He wore a very conservative black suit, white shirt, vest, and tie.

"Marshal Long," the president said, holding out his hand. "I'd heard you were in town and was hoping I might meet you. Nothing official, of course. One of your fellow marshals did yeoman work tracking down the men who robbed our bank two years ago. Found them over in Texas, but the cash was all gone."

"Glad to hear that they were caught," Longarm said. "I have a few questions to ask you, if you have the time, Mr. Leslie."

"Always have time for lawmen. Come into my office, where we'll have some privacy."

Jennifer had stayed in the background as Longarm first talked to the banker. Now the two men went into the president's office and the door closed.

"I understand you're here to work on the Wallace Johnson killing, Mr. Long."

"That's one of my projects. I'm also here on a warrant concerning a banking problem. That's where I hope you can help me."

"A banking crime?"

"Not done here. There was a check that passed through your bank and found its way into some stolen goods. If I gave you the date and name of the signer, could you tell me anything about the draft?"

"I only wish we could, Marshal Long. We deal with dozens of checks and drafts every day. Was this recently?"

"I'm afraid the draft was dated over a year ago."

"Not a chance. We don't keep a record of accounts after six months. A copy is sent to the account holder, and we have to make room for more records. Finding one individual check written a year ago would be virtually impossible for us. We're a small bank and don't have the services that some of those Denver banks do."

"Well, Mr. Leslie, I guess that takes care of my questions. The Denver banks told us not to have much hope."

"What will you do then?"

"Pursue the culprit in another manner. We have some other leads and some evidence that we'll check over again. I'd say that I've taken enough of your time, Mr. Leslie. Thanks for your help. I hope you don't need our services any more on a bank robbery."

"My fondest hope as well, Marshal Long."

They said good-bye and Longarm ambled toward the front door. Jennifer had headed out the same way a dozen feet before Longarm got there. She met him on the sidewalk.

"Is he the killer?"

"He's a banker. That would be the perfect job for an embezzler who stole money from one bank. He could start his own bank. Unfortunately, banker Leslie doesn't look like the type to be either an embezzler or a killer. I'd put him far down on my suspect list. He's rich, doesn't go to church, must have a buggy and a house, but that's about it.

"So what are we supposed to do now? We've run out of rich suspects."

"We keep looking," Longarm said.

"Not before I have a cup of coffee or at least a mug of soup for dinner. It's almost twelve noon and I'm starved."

They ate in the café they had frequented several times before and had soup and sandwiches. When they went to the street after the meal, Jennifer caught the marshal's arm.

"Time to have that bandage changed. Dr. Smith said to come back in two days, and that was three or four days ago. Does it hurt?"

"Of course it hurts. Any gunshot wound hurts, but this one isn't that bad. If no one reminds me of it, I forget about it."

"Then let's get the dressing changed and some new medicine put on it so it'll heal up fast."

Before Longarm could complain too loudly, they were at Dr. Amos Smith's office, and Jennifer led him into the small waiting room. A nurse came to the door. Jennifer said they needed a dressing changed, and the woman went out the same door.

"Doesn't really need changing. We're just taking up the doctor's time when he should be with sick people."

Before Longarm could bolt for the door, Dr. Smith stuck his head out and motioned. Jennifer was behind him and Longarm felt trapped. He went into the small room with no complaint, but once there and with Jennifer in the waiting room, he made his try.

"Dr. Smith, I know you're busy, and so am I. Jennifer insisted that I come. You just wrap some clean bandage around my arm and we'll call it square."

"Does the arm hurt?"

"A little."

"No long running lines of red coming from it?"

"Not a one, Doctor."

"Why don't I just cut off the old bandage, put on some more ointment, and then rewrap it? Won't take but five minutes."

Longarm had been pushed enough. "No, Doctor. I said it was fine. I don't know how I let her drag me in here. When you take off the old bandage, it'll hurt like hell for two hours, and right now I don't need that. Forget it. You go and talk to somebody who really needs your services. No offense, but sometimes a man has to put his foot down."

Dr. Smith chuckled. "Having a time with our Jennifer, I see. She's a tough one when she wants to be. But the best schoolmarm this town has had in at least five years. I'll wrap it twice and make it look new."

He did the deed and Longarm thanked him. He hurried out to Jennifer and showed her the clean bandage, and she was satisfied.

"That's going to make it feel a lot better, you just wait and see."

They walked down the boardwalk, on the way to the schoolmarm's house.

"Time to look at those clues. Wally must have thought I could figure them out, but I'm not what you'd call a good puzzle solver. Never have been. Logic I'm good at, but puzzles leave me feeling stupid."

They were a block from the sheriff's office when Longarm heard gunfire. A deputy ran out of the front door and looked both ways, then raced up the street in Longarm's direction. He seemed to be looking for someone, as he checked people on the street, quickly scanned those in stores, and then hurried on. When he was fifty feet from Longarm, he bellowed in delight.

"Hey, Marshal Long. Sheriff wants to see you right away. Urgent." He looked at Jennifer. "Best to leave the lady here."

Longarm directed Jennifer to stay and hurried away with the deputy sheriff. Halfway to the office the deputy looked over and frowned.

"Know that gent you brought in for murder, the one from the grave robbers?"

"Remember him well, Phil Noonan."

"The son of a bitch just killed one of our deputies and escaped out the back door. Sheriff wants you to come along on a manhunt for the bastard!"

Chapter 14

Longarm ran with the sheriff's deputy toward the jail. "How long ago did Noonan break out?"

"We're not sure. He overpowered Charlie and we didn't know it. We went to check and found Charlie with his throat slit and his shotgun and revolver gone. Damn killer could have been missing for up to two hours."

Longarm grabbed a Spencer repeating rifle as they ran through the sheriff's office and out the back. Someone had brought saddled horses. There were six men ready to ride. Longarm and the other deputy made eight.

The sheriff stood and waved at them. "Go get the bastard. Since this was Longarm's prisoner, I'm making him head of the hunt. Answer to his say-so. He knows what he's doing."

Sheriff Murdock walked over to where Longarm was checking the saddle and the girth on his horse.

"We usually keep two horses saddled back here," he said as Longarm mounted. "One of them is missing. One of my men checked for prints and found a set heading from our lean-to west out the alley. I'd say those are the killer's tracks."

Longarm nodded.

"Who found the sign?" he called.

"Yo, Deputy Elder," one of the men sang out and rode up.

"We'll follow them on foot until we get him out of town," Longarm said, stepping off his mount. Deputy Elder dropped off as well, and the two headed down the alley, leading their horses, one on each side of the set of prints.

Soon they found spurts of sand and dirt behind the prints. Noonan had lifted the horse to a run right there in the alley.

It took them twenty minutes to track the animal through three blocks of town. The killer had kept to the alleys, which made it simpler to follow him, since there was little traffic in those areas. When they saw that the horse and rider had headed out a side road that led generally west, toward the mountains, the two trackers mounted their horses and began leapfrogging each other to check the trail.

They determined the general direction the rider had taken; then Longarm rode ahead at a gallop for a quarter of a mile, got off his horse, and worked back and forth across the suspected trail at right angles until he found the prints. When he was sure they were the same ones, he signaled the rest of the search party, which had been working ahead slowly, following the trail.

Then Deputy Elder rode a quarter of a mile out, found the trail, and called up the rest.

In this way they could speed up the tracking process tenfold.

The route led upward, through some ponderosa groves along the slopes of a ravine, then up and over a hogback. The tracking slowed as they came to more rugged country. There they walked to find the trail, leading their horses behind them.

The fugitive had no supplies, no food. Why was he working higher and higher into the mountains? Longarm had thought that he would hit the South Road toward Santa Fe and try to get his trail confused with other hoofprints and wagon tracks on the roadway.

Still Noonan worked higher.

They trailed the man through the blue spruce now, and Douglas fir on the higher slopes. Once they came to a sharp rise where the horse evidently had slipped and skidded down some sheet rock. They found blood on the rocks.

"Coulda come from either the man or the horse," Longarm opined. "Truth is we'll all be a-walking from here on."

Just before the trail reached a sheer cliff rising a hundred feet, it turned downward and angled toward a heavy growth of blue spruce.

"Leastwise he's heading in the right direction," Longarm said.

They followed the trail the rest of the afternoon. The killer's head start and the route he had traveled made it a slow tracking game. Noonan was getting farther and farther ahead of them. As the sun slid behind the far western mountain peaks, Longarm called a halt and tried to figure it.

"He come all the way up here, and now he's heading down again. I'd bet my bonnet that the South Road to Santa Fe can't be more than another five miles or so away."

He pondered it a minute then turned to the rest of the posse. "I want two men to get from here to the South Road and patrol a stretch about five miles long. Watch for this Noonan. He might be hitting the trail and heading south."

Two men held up hands and Longarm nodded. "You know how to get to the South Road before dark?"

"Hell yes, Marshal. I lived in these parts for ten years now."

"Get moving."

Longarm stared at the angle the trail had taken ahead. He didn't like splitting up a posse any more than needed. But right here two men could do as well as six.

"Chances are Noonan will keep moving after dark. That means we don't stand a chance in a chicken coop of catching him." Longarm pondered it, then remembered another time, another chase. He grinned.

"You men with rifles. I want each of you to put four shots into the woods. Aim them up ahead and careful not to shoot where our two deputies just rode. Space the shots out a little."

For the next five minutes, rifles blasted into the quiet of the high-country forest. When silence returned, one of the deputies frowned.

"Marshal, what the hell was that for?"

"I'm grabbing at lifelines here, Deputy. With any luck one of those rounds will come close enough to Noonan to make him rush along a little faster. This close to dark, a horse or a man can make a little mistake that turns into something big."

"Like a horse hurting a leg?" the deputy asked.

"About the size of it."

They remained quiet for a moment. No one heard a thing.

136

Longarm went back to reading sign. Working through the soft undergrowth made for easy tracking. For fifty or sixty years the pine needles had fallen off the evergreens and made a carpet, then a rotting and disintegrating mulch, on the forest floor.

Where there wasn't an expanse of rock, the hoofprints of Noonan's animal were easy to follow. But it was slow work.

It was near dusk and they were about a half mile farther down the gentle slope of the mountain when Longarm pulled his mount to a halt.

"Hear that?" he asked.

It came again, the high keening, the terrible scream of a horse in unimaginable agony. Then far ahead of them they heard a single revolver shot and the screaming stopped.

"Got him!" Longarm bellowed. "Not saying that our rifle shots scared Noonan so much he made a mistake with his mount, but it might have helped. A little luck always comes in handy for a lawman. Now, new strategy."

He called to Deputy Elder. Before the two left, he gave instructions to the four deputy sheriffs remaining.

"Elder and I will move ahead on foot. At first light you follow us best you can and trail our horses. My guess is that Noonan will keep moving tonight in the dark even after his horse went down. Just what direction, I don't know. Our hope is that he'll continue downhill and try for the South Road. If you lose us, we'll all meet on the South Road. If we aren't there by tomorrow noon, wait for us. If we get Noonan, we'll give you three quick rifle shots. Got that?"

The deputies said they understood.

Longarm and Elder took their rifles and headed out on foot. Longarm moved with ease through the ponderosa forest. It grew at the forty-five to eighty-five-hundred-foot elevations. That meant less underbrush, easier traveling.

The deputy United States marshal set a fast pace as they worked downhill and through the ponderosa. There was a scrap of a moon, but not much of the light got through the trees. At times they could see no more than ten feet ahead of them.

In one place they came to a razorback ridge. Longarm picked the right-hand side, and they slid down to the base and then worked down to what proved to be a small valley, maybe a

137

hundred yards wide at the top. Here there was grass and no trees, and the two men made good time.

About halfway down the valley they stopped and listened. They could hear nothing but a night bird's cry now and then, small feet scuttering through the grass and weeds, and the gentle rustling of the wind through the trees at the edge of the meadow.

"If he's out here, he's damn quiet," Longarm said. "He's too smart to make a fire and get warm. Wood smoke would rattle my cranium from five miles away if'n I was downwind."

"So where do we go now?"

"Let's sit a spell and listen. Might get a clue."

After a half hour on Longarm's Waterbury they hadn't heard a thing, so they moved on down the valley, their rifles getting heavier by the yard.

"Tired?" Longarm asked Elder.

"Yeah."

"So is Noonan. I figure by now we're past him. What we need to do is find ourselves a handy spot we can watch from and wait him out until morning. My thinking is that he figures he's ahead of us because we can't track him at night. He must guess he has enough of a start on us so he can get to the South Road early in the morning and pick up a ride with the stage or maybe some wagon going that direction."

"So where do we hole up?"

"How about in the woods right over yonder? It'll give us a good view of the whole sweep of the little valley. I figure it's more than a mile long. Be a magnet for him to use after crashing brush and pine trees half of the night."

They walked to the edge of the valley and found low brush, a few looming ponderosa pine, and an open space where they could stretch out.

"We'll be concealed by the brush, but still able to see through it," Longarm said.

Deputy Sheriff Elder squatted near the federal lawman. "You want me to stand the first watch?"

"Ain't needed, Elder. If that varmint comes within a hundred yards of us, I'll be up bright-eyed and have my sights on him. Just sack out there and have a snooze. My guess is that we're gonna need all the strength we have tomorrow. I didn't figure this Noonan was such a good woodsman. We'll have to be ready tomorrow. You say he has a shotgun, but no rifle."

"We didn't find a rifle missing. He just grabbed the scattergun we keep back by the cells and took Charlie's sixer."

"Good, we have him outgunned. Now get some rest."

Longarm pushed his hat down over his eyes, laced his fingers together under his head, and went to sleep.

The federal lawman roused sometime after midnight. He heard a pair of big cats screaming at each other, but they were a half mile away. Those cougars could make all sorts of noise when they were fighting. Or were they mating? He didn't know.

When Longarm woke up next, streaks of light stabbed into the eastern sky. He scanned the valley, but it was too dark yet. They would wait until nine o'clock. If Noonan didn't show up by then, they would figure he'd got around them.

Deputy Elder came awake at dawn. Together they watched the north end of the valley. Nothing moved.

Then something did. A pair of does and two fawns ambled out of the brush and nibbled at the tender shoots of new grass in the meadow. One doe stood sentry duty as the other one grazed. Then the first one ate and the second one watched.

Ten minutes later, they bounded to the center of the valley, where a stripe of green showed the splash of a small stream. As Longarm watched the does and their young, he saw the head of one of the females snap upward, her ears straining to the north.

A fraction of a second later the does were pushing the young fawns toward the far edge of the brush. They bounced away, then came back to hurry the youngsters. Just before they vanished into the woods, a man stepped out of the edge of the timber at the north end of the valley, a half mile away.

"Aha!" Longarm said. "He's ours." But before he could bring up his Spencer to wait for a shot, the man faded back into the brush, out of sight.

"Smarter than we thought," Deputy Elder said. "He must figure some of us got past him in the night. So which side will he come down?"

"He's closest to this side. Let's hope he comes this way. But to stop him short, Elder, I want you to take off in the brush here and go down to the end of the valley and see if you can get across to the woods on the far side without showing yourself. If you can, find a spot over there to block him if he tries to come that way. Did the sheriff say this was a shoot-to-kill operation?"

"Damn right. He killed Charlie, one of ours. We got to kill him to even the score. Saves the county money that way, too."

"Right. Get moving."

Elder nodded, held his rifle at port arms, and jogged downstream through the timber.

Longarm changed his spot. He found a ponderosa that was three feet thick at the base and sat down behind it. He cleared away some small brush and grass so he could peer around either side of the monster tree and see for nearly forty yards straight up that side of the timber next to the valley. It was the best he could do. He chambered a round in the Spencer and waited.

A half mile shouldn't take more than ten minutes to walk, Longarm figured. Time half gone. He lay on his belly and stared out the cleared space on the right side of the ponderosa. It had been a good night's sleep, but some country-fried potatoes, three eggs sunny side up, a rasher of bacon, and three cups of Arbuckle sure would go good about now.

He waited. After what he figured had been another five minutes, he looked up the side of the valley again. Nothing showed in his view. He had heard no movement at all. Was this Noonan that good a woodsman that he could slip right past?

Longarm stood so he could get a higher angle and peered around the left side of the ponderosa with just his eyes and forehead showing. Twenty yards ahead he saw some tall grass and low brush move. Something was there. The wind didn't penetrate the valley.

He watched the spot again. More movement. A man on his belly? A red fox, maybe a coyote?

He ducked back out of sight and pondered the situation. A crash of brush to the far left, almost at the valley grass, jolted Longarm to bring up the Spencer and search for a target. Nothing there.

The old throw-a-rock-to-make-noise trick, Longarm decided. He changed directions and checked all of the area to the right of where he had seen the man before.

He scanned the area of brush, small ponderosa, and leaf-and-pine-needle mulch. There! Movement. The flick of a brown-shirted arm to pull in behind a two-foot ponderosa. Longarm brought up the Spencer and sighted in at ground level on the right side of the tree. A head showed momentarily, then vanished. No time to trigger a shot.

If Noonan had seen him, had seen the rifle, he'd be more careful now, use greater stealth.

To Longarm's surprise, Noonan fired a shot of the lawman double-aught buckshot at the big ponderosa and took off running full speed through the trees and brush, heading south.

Longarm tried to get off a shot. Too much brush, too many trees. A twig the size of your finger could throw a rifle round off a foot.

He brought the Spencer down and raced after Noonan. He had to remember the damn shotgun. In here it was a more deadly weapon than a rifle or a six-gun. Those double-aught rounds each carried lawman loads of seventeen .32-caliber balls. Enough to blow a man in half at ten feet.

He ran.

Longarm could hear the killer racing ahead of him. Then suddenly the noise stopped. Longarm halted at once and dropped to one knee. He listened. Not an alien sound. Only a cricket, two squalling jays, and far off the hooting of some mourning doves.

The time stretched out. Longarm had learned to wait from the masters, the Indians. He eased the rifle up so it aimed front, and searched nearby with his eyes to find some cover from which Noonan might suddenly lift up and get off the first round. There was no protective cover. No first round for Noonan.

Then a blur in front of him moved. Longarm lifted and fired, aiming automatically, then flapped the trigger guard down and back up on the Spencer to ram a new round into the firing chamber. He came out of his kneeling position, clawing air as he raced forward.

Now he caught a flash of the brown shirt ahead. He fired again, heard a wail, and knew he had cut flesh. How bad the wound was he didn't know. The crashing continued.

Slowly Longarm closed the gap on the double killer. In the sudden rush, a new element emerged. From south somewhere,

Longarm heard a rifle bark and a round slam through the brush near where he guessed Noonan had dropped.

"Bastards!" Noonan screamed.

"Give it up, Noonan, and live. You'll get a fair trial in Taos."

"Fair, sure, I knocked off a lawman. I'll get hung in Taos."

He fired the shotgun again, and only Longarm's belly-down position saved him. He felt one of the slugs nip off three standing hairs on his head.

The rifle from below, handled by Deputy Elder, snarled again, and Noonan bleated in pain.

"Bastards! Damn rifle. You and me are a good match, but that damn rifleman is off a hundred yards peppering me."

"Give it up and face trial, Noonan. Better than going down this way."

"Hell, what's the difference? This way I don't have to worry about that damn hangman."

There was a silence then. Longarm hoped Noonan was reconsidering.

"Hell, maybe you're right. You the one they call Longarm?"

The deputy marshal almost answered, but he smelled a trap. He dove to the left and rolled behind a fallen ponderosa log just as the rain of deadly .32 rounds slammed through the air, chewing up the ground where he had been seconds before.

At the end of his roll, Longarm had whipped the cross-draw .44–40 out of his holster, lifted over the log, and fired three times at Noonan, who had jumped to the side of a tree and stood to get the higher angle.

One of the rounds slammed into Noonan's left shoulder, and he bellowed in pain and darted behind three big pines. Then he charged south, running hard.

Longarm surged to his feet and stormed after him, the rifle up, the Colt back in leather. Twice more he nearly had a shot at the killer, but brush intervened. Then the crashing sounds stopped, and Longarm darted behind the closest ponderosa and waited. His ragged breathing evened and slowed.

"You ready to give up, Noonan?"

There was no response. Longarm went low on the tree and looked around, a foot off the leaf mold. He could see part of Noonan's leg angling from behind a tree thirty feet ahead. Not much of a shot.

Longarm steadied the Spencer and was about to pull the trigger when the leg vanished. At almost the same time a rifle shot came from ahead somewhere and thunked into the pine wood.

"Damn bastards!" Noonan screamed.

Longarm checked the country behind him. They were at the end of the brush along the meadow. It widened here, and directly behind Noonan was six or eight feet of trees and brush and then nothing but foot-high grass waving in the morning breeze.

Noonan was trapped.

The shotgun roared, and Longarm saw Deputy Elder edging into the brush. Some of the seventeen slugs went wide and hit branches and brush, but enough got through and slammed Elder backward into the grass, which hid him.

Noonan screeched in delight.

Longarm heard the metallic snap as Noonan broke open the shotgun. Noonan hadn't loaded the double-barreled weapon after he fired the first round. Now it was dry. Longarm charged the thirty feet toward the pine. He could hear the frantic juggling as Noonan tried to load the scattergun.

Then it was too late. Longarm blasted around the tree and slammed into the outlaw killer with his shoulder, jolting the shotgun out of his hands. Longarm and Noonan fell into the brush and grass and rolled once. Longarm had his arms around the killer and pinned him to the ground for a moment.

Noonan kicked hard with one knee, and Longarm had to cover up his crotch and slide to the left, which gave Noonan the leverage he needed to break Longarm's bear hug.

Both men spun apart, and each darted a hand for his six-gun. Longarm's hand came up empty. His Colt had been scraped out of the cross-draw rig.

Noonan drew his revolver just as Longarm dove at him. The lawman caught the rising six-gun, his big hand grabbing the cylinder so it couldn't turn.

The muzzle pointed directly at Longarm's chest, but without the cylinder, the hammer wouldn't come back and fall and the weapon couldn't fire.

Slowly Longarm forced the muzzle of the weapon away from his chest. Gradually he bent it around, farther and farther, until the six-gun's muzzle pointed at Noonan's chest. In one quick move Longarm released his hand around the cylinder but kept the revolver aimed at Noonan. When Noonan realized that the cylinder was free, it was too late to reduce his finger's pressure on the trigger. The cylinder turned and the weapon fired.

The round spun out of the short barrel into Noonan's chest, missed his heart, lacerated a lung, and dug holes through two large arteries.

The killer dropped the weapon and caught his chest.

"No! It wasn't supposed to end this way! No!"

Longarm grabbed the six-gun and searched the grass until he found his own Colt. Then he frisked Noonan. He had no other weapon, not even a boot knife.

Longarm ran to where Deputy Elder lay. The lawman was alive.

"Damn, Longarm, he nicked me. About four of them double-aught slugs caught me. One bad one in the chest. Rest don't matter. Take a look."

Longarm checked the deputy's shirt. It showed a ring of blood. He unbuttoned it and chuckled.

"You're the luckiest man still alive, Elder. That slug must have been almost spent going through a branch. It hit a rib and plowed sideways for about an inch just under the skin and caused blood all over the place, but no real damage. You ain't dead; you can get up and walk now."

They both went back and watched the dying man beside the ponderosa. He sweat and swore. He screamed at the pain, and then he looked so peaceful they didn't believe it. A moment later he bellowed in rage at them and tried to sit up, only to make one last, low cry for help and slump back to the bloodstained grass, dead in a trice.

Longarm looked at Deputy Elder.

"That evens the score. Now, do you have any idea where the South Road and our mounts are?"

"Matter of fact, I do. I could see part of it from where I went around the bottom of the valley. It's no more than a half mile beyond that spot."

Longarm nodded. "No sense making you walk out. We'll tie up those scratches."

He took the Spencer and fired three quick rounds into the air. "The boys should be here with our horses from one side or the other in fifteen minutes. With any luck we'll have you back to town by noon and get you doctored up."

Chapter 15

Longarm saw Jennifer pacing up and down in front of the Sheriff's office as he and his posse turned down Main Street. She looked up, saw the eight riders coming, and hurried down the street, her long skirt brushing the boardwalk. She ran the last half block until the moment when he figured she must have identified him riding at the head of the pack.

Then she stopped and waited for the riders. When they came up to her, she paced them along the sidewalk. A big smile broke over her face when she saw that Longarm had no additional bandages on his body.

He left the dead man facedown over a saddle with the sheriff and rode with Deputy Elder down to the doctor's office. Longarm escorted Elder inside and told the nurse to take good care of him; then he hurried outside and caught the Indian girl's hand.

"Now, pretty Indian maiden, I hope you missed me. I'm in dire need of a hot bath, a big dinner, a long nap, a big supper, and then a whole lot of loving. Do you think that can be arranged?"

"Yes. Maybe, but I'll have to buy some things. I need one of those new iceboxes. You might tell the school board. Let me go to the store." She was smiling, her black hair bobbing with every step, her dark eyes shining in her pretty Indian face.

"I need to talk to the sheriff a mite; then I'll be coming down to your place. Oh, I never did take my traveling bags down there, did I? I'll bring them from the hotel. No use paying good money for lodging when I can sponge off the locals."

He waved and walked the mount back to the sheriff's office. His talk with the lawman inside was short.

"Sheriff, we trailed him. Your men were a big help, especially Deputy Elder. He took four double-aught buck slugs but won't have even a scar to show for it. All his wounds are superficial. When we caught up with Noonan, he wouldn't surrender. His damn shotgun was wicked.

"Finally rushed him, got rid of the scattergun, but he had out his sixer. I grabbed it around the cylinder so it wouldn't fire and finally pointed it at him. I suddenly let go of the cylinder and the pressure he had on the trigger pulled it without him wanting it to. The round killed him. Saved the country the cost of a trial and a hanging.

"You're welcome. Now I'm heading for a big dinner and a bath and a long nap. If you want me, wait until tomorrow."

An hour later, Longarm had just finished the big dinner Jennifer Walking Dove had cooked on her wood-burning stove in the schoolmarm's house. He'd eaten ham slices, new potatoes, and peas in a cheese sauce, along with slabs of fresh-baked bread and enough Arbuckle to sink a battleship. The apple pie came out last, with slices of yellow cheese on the side and a big spread of whipped cream on top.

He kissed her quickly and dove into the apple pie. "Pretty lady, you can cook for me just any old time you want to. Maybe I'll bundle you up and take you along in my Gladstone, unfolding you at every stop to do the cooking." He grinned. "And, of course, other sexy things a woman is wont to do."

"You haven't told me about it. Did you get shot at? At least you didn't get wounded."

"Don't need to tell you about it. All over. What I'm hoping is that I don't drown when I have my bath in that short tub the school board provided you. Did I put on enough water? Is it hot yet?"

He got a yes to both questions and finished a quarter of the pie before he carried the buckets and a copper boiler full of hot water to the small bathroom, where the tub stood solidly against the wall.

"Do I get to help you with your bath?"

"Little darling, in or out of the tub, it's fine with me. But I'm warning you, I didn't get much sleep last night and I need that nap before I get serious about lovemaking."

"Don't need to get serious, just a quick one to kind of keep me from crawling all over you when you try to get to sleep."

He poured the water in the tub and tested it. Too hot. He put in another bucket of water from the pitcher pump on the back porch.

He left it too hot so it would stay hot longer, then stripped and stood there for her inspection.

"Dirt, sweat, and saddle sores," he explained as he stepped into the tub and reached for the bar of lye soap he found in the soap dish.

She watched his privates vanish under the water and gave a soft cry of alarm. "Please don't let him drown down there."

"That big guy swims like a fish. He'll be fine. Sure you don't want to join me?"

"Not just for a bath. I've bathed before. Now if you want to do some serious sexy business . . ."

"Later, when I smell better."

"At least I get to watch."

"Feel free to do that."

He attacked the grime of the two-day ride with the strong soap and now and then looked at the lovely Indian girl. He saw with surprise that she was taking her clothes off. A moment later she was as naked as he was and sitting on a chair. Her eyes went half closed and slowly her hands began to caress and fondle her breasts. She made soft sounds as she worked on her orbs. Then one hand slid down her side, massaging her soft, white flesh as her murmurings rose. A minute later both hands moved down and massaged her legs, then fondled her tender inner thighs next to her crotch.

He stopped washing and watched her. Her eyes were closed, her neck stretched upward to lift her head high as if she were looking at the ceiling.

Small sounds came from her. One hand went back and concentrated on a breast, and soon the orb was glowing and her nipple rising with full, hot blood.

"Oh, yes!" she moaned softly. Then the words were gone and the sounds were more like those of a contented she-bear in heat.

Longarm washed slowly, watching her. Her legs spread where she sat on the chair facing him. Her legs went wider and wider, and then one hand went back to her tender inner thighs and she massaged them. One at a time.

Her top hand now worked on her other breast, building it up to white-hot heat.

When she had caressed both her inner thighs, her fingers darted over her crotch, which he could see was open, her pink nether lips smiling at him.

"Ohhhhhhhhhhhhhhhhhhhhh yes!" she crooned as she stroked across her tender heartland. "Good, so good!" Her finger found the hard little node hiding near her lips, and she stroked it. Her whole body jerked and shivered. She stroked it again and rolled her eyes and moaned with such feeling and depth that Longarm wanted to jump out of the water and put an end to her wanting by mounting her right there on the chair.

Twice more her finger twanged the clit, and after the second time she trembled, then started to shake and spin herself into the kind of climaxes he knew so well.

Her whole body vibrated and shivered. Her legs spasmed and cramped, and her arm and hand muscles contracted as her hips humped forward again and again, as if to capture more of the penis that surely must be poking into her.

The vibrations increased and surged and became stronger. She nearly fell off the chair but grabbed the back with one hand as her other hand now left her clit and pushed three fingers into her vagina as far as they would go. Then she began her own poking, a dozen times, then again, until at last she climaxed once more.

This time it was the long, braying howl of a wild animal, announcing to the world that nature was good and that the animal world was replenishing itself, that life would go on.

When the wailing stopped, she dropped her hands and closed her knees and her head sagged all the way to her thighs. She sat that way for five minutes without moving.

Longarm finished his bath and stepped out of the tub, drying himself quickly. He was only half-dry when he picked up the Indian girl in both arms and carried her to her bed. He laid her down and she stretched out. For a moment her eyes remained closed; then they opened one at a time and she smiled tentatively.

"Nobody else but you has ever seen me do that. It's a tension reliever now and then. Sometimes I don't find a man I want to make love to for six months at a time."

"Why now?"

"I guess I was hurt that you didn't want me to jump in the bath and screw you. One of my little problems. Do you want me now?"

"Does a hog like slop?"

She grinned and patted the bed beside her. They came together gently, softly, and for the first time with this woman, Longarm figured that this was what married love would be like. Total familiarity with each other. Knowing what the other person liked and wanted and what she didn't want to do. At ease, relaxed; soft and wonderful.

When they finished, she held him tight and whispered in his ear.

"Again. Get him hard for me and do me again right quick. How fast can you get him up again?

"I've never used a stopwatch on my regenerative powers," Longarm said laughing.

"Then let's try." She looked at the windup alarm clock by the side of the bed. "It's two-thirty-one, and we're timing this."

They lay on their sides, still connected. She brought one of his hands up to her breasts and then kissed him, the long, slow, deliberate kind intended to make a man bulge his Sunday pants.

She used her inside muscles, squeezing him, gripping and relaxing, gripping and relaxing.

"You trying to saw me in half, woman?"

She grinned. "Just an old Indian trick I learned at boarding school."

A few moments later she looked at the clock. "It's two-thirty-five. You should be more than ready by now."

Longarm chuckled. He was ready. "You have a suggestion?"

"You on top fast and furious and hard, and don't wait for me, just plow ahead and get your own satisfaction the best and quickest way you can."

"Still might take a while. I ain't no sixteen year old."

"I'm glad." She rolled over on her back, pulling away from him, then spread her knees and lifted her legs high.

"Do me fast!"

Longarm dove right in. He was surprised how fast he came, considering all of the preliminaries and since this was his second or third time—he wasn't sure.

It was a smashing, going-down-in-flames session that climaxed with both of them making it at the same time and the small house shaking with their grunts and screams and bellows of delight.

When their lust cooled, they settled on the bed side by side and watched each other.

"I'm not going to be glad when you find Wally's killer," Jennifer said. "That means you'll be leaving soon, and you won't take me along, in a kit bag or on a horse."

"Sorry, Little Dove, that's the way things are. You knew that the first time you opened your blouse and showed me your goods."

"Yes, but I am a woman, and I can still sorrow for the day I don't want to come." She snuggled close to him. "You still want that nap?"

He shook his head. "Let's get dressed and take a small walk. I want to kick around some of the clues again about who the hell our killer embezzler is. It's got to be there right in front of our faces."

They dressed and walked around the town. When they passed the doctor's office, Jennifer looked at the lawman's wounds. "Shouldn't you have the doctor look at your hurts?"

"We were just here yesterday or the day before. My arm feels fine. It's healing. Sometimes a wound gets healed up faster if there ain't a lot of poking and fussing with it."

"Old Indian remedy."

"That new clue, the smell, and those two flat, short sticks I found outside of the place where that bushwhacker tried to nail me, both bother me a lot. It's like they're the clues we should be concerned with, but nothing comes. Sticks and a smell. If I could only figure out where that smell came from, I'd feel

150

a lot better. When that happens, we just might have ourselves the name of the killer."

They walked around town, and Longarm found himself sniffing more than ever before in his life. He sensed the acrid smell of urine behind a horse, the dusty odor of an old tarp over a wagon of goods. He sensed the vibrant mountain air with a twang in it that came from the pine trees.

But nowhere did he capture the one particular smell that he was trying to find. Where the hell was it?

They wound up back at the kitchen table with all eighteen of the clues spread out. The first six were for a rich man, that was for sure. The next six were tougher. The saw, the book, the newborn baby, the rattlesnake, the picture of Main Street, and a church with a heavy X through it. To Longarm the series still didn't make a lot of sense. A non-churchman, maybe one who struck like a rattlesnake and couldn't be trusted. But a book and a newborn baby? Both left him frustrated.

Saws. There were all kinds of saws. Once he'd seen a man saw a steel pipe in half with a hacksaw; another time he'd seen a country barber, where there was no doctor, saw off a man's leg to keep him alive.

Books. Almost everyone could read a little. Books were all around. He'd noticed the fledgling Taos library on one of his walks. They were asking for contributions of books no longer needed.

Longarm didn't want to look at the third set of clues. They were harder yet.

While he pondered the pictures, Jennifer went into her bedroom. When she came out, she had on her doeskin ceremonial dress and her black hair was in two short braids at the sides of her head.

"Hey, white eye, you want to make the love with shy Indian virgin?"

Longarm laughed until his side ached. He grabbed her and kissed her, and she led him outside. "Once more out in the woods. I know a fine spot upstream beyond the Pueblo village. We can get there in five minutes. That is if you want to poke a real Indian pussy with that big long cock of yours."

"Yeah, damned if I don't want to. Lead on to the poking, woman. Been a long time since I got to screw a real Indian gal in her doeskin. You got any surprises under that skirt?"

"White man will have to wait and see."

It took them fifteen minutes to find the right spot. A gaggle of Indian boys and girls were splashing in the water and playing games where Jennifer first wanted to sex down.

They found another place where they could see the water, and she spread out the blanket she had carried from the house. Longarm lay back on it, and she grinned and dropped beside him.

"Can I tell you a romantic old Pueblo Indian legend?"

"If it isn't more than an hour long."

"Good. This old Pueblo Indian legend is about a virgin girl of fifteen who is wading in a shallow stream and finds a bullfrog on the bank. The frog is not afraid of her. She picks up the frog, and to her surprise it talks to her in her native tongue.

"The frog asks her if she thinks he's pretty, and she says for a frog he's about the prettiest thing she's ever seen. He croaks his pleasure. Then the frog does a strange thing. He asks her if she will kiss him.

"Now, this is a surprise for the Indian girl, so she frowns and says she's never kissed a frog before. She's never even kissed an Indian boy before. The frog pleads and says it won't be so hard. He promises her a big surprise if she'll kiss him right on his lips.

"She asks him what kind of a surprise, but he won't tell her. He says she'll be happy with it, he guarantees it.

"They talk about it all afternoon, and she plays in the water, and the frog jumps in and swims around her and comes to rest on her full bosom, which is just barely underwater.

"The girl says that feels strange. He says kiss him and she'll be truly surprised and pleased and happy for the rest of her life. He's so insistent, and such a gentleman frog, that she picks him up, holds him high, stares him right in his green eyes, and kisses his green lips.

"At once there is a great hissing, and the frog leaps to the far shore, and there before her eyes he turns into a handsome Pueblo Indian warrior of twenty years.

"She hurries from the water, and he takes her in his arms and kisses her properly, and she falls in love with him, and they are married and live for a hundred years and are so happy they tell everyone the story."

Longarm grinned. "What a strange yarn. Is it really one of the old, old tales of the Pueblo storyteller?"

"It is, and I believe every word of it."

"Good, because I'm an ugly frog and I want to kiss you."

"I was hoping you would."

The kiss lasted a long time, and when it was over, her Indian dress was up around her chin and the rest of her naked body had been thoroughly fondled by Longarm's talented and wandering hands.

She undressed him, and they lay there side by side, naked and wanting each other.

"How this time?" Longarm asked.

"Like the frog," she said, laughing. "You sit up and put your legs out in front. Then I come and face you and sit down."

"Well, girl, it just might work," Longarm opined.

He moved into position, and she worked toward him, putting one leg on each side of his hips and both hands around his neck as she lowered slowly toward his lance-hard erection.

Longarm guided both of them, and with the first penetration, Jennifer let out a whoop of delight.

"I knew it would work. I just knew it!" As she slid down on his turgid shaft, she rumbled with delight; then she cried out in victory when they settled together in total unison and could go no farther.

"I'm kind of pinned to the blanket here, woman. You get the honor of doing most of the work."

At once she lifted up an inch and went back down, then she moved up higher and slid down. After several tries she found the right distance and set up a rhythm that worked faster on Longarm than any position he could remember. In two or three minutes he was so worked up he couldn't hold back and bellowed in roaring approval as he punched his hips upward, jetting his load into her and bringing a wail of delightful loss from Jennifer.

She worked faster then, and soon her own satisfaction powered through her body, and she writhed and shifted her weight as they both rolled to the blanket, on their sides, where she reached the crashing, shivering, vibrating end of her third climax.

They lay bound together for a moment, then eased apart. She nestled against him. "Why am I so afraid that you'll be leaving me before long?"

"Intuition, a woman's way of knowing things that she has no hard facts to prove. That kind of thinking gets us men into trouble all the time."

"Then you will be leaving?"

"After we get this killer and embezzler brought to justice. First we have to figure out who he is."

"So we have a few more days. I'm working on those clues as hard as I can, I assure you."

"We both are."

"Once more. I want to be on top again. You'd be surprised how many men won't let a woman be on top. Lots of the women tell me this. I'm not sure why they confide in me. Trying to shock me, I guess. Did you know that women talk a lot about sex when they get together and there are no men around? We do. We certainly do."

They made love again, and she shrieked when she climaxed, riding him like a young buffalo on a she-cow. Then they came apart and splashed in the stream for a few minutes. The water was cold. Much of it came from melting snow high in the mountains or from ice-fed springs.

Later they lay on the blanket, drying off in the sun.

"Will you ever come back this way, Custis Long?"

"Now and then. I've been through Taos before on my work."

"When you come, be sure and find me. I'll probably be the schoolteacher here for a long time. They don't seem anxious to find another one, and I can teach the whites and Mexicans and my own people.

"I've set up a school for the Pueblo children to start this fall. It will begin when the regular school lets out. I have to furnish all my own materials, but the school board will let us use the schoolhouse and the stove and wood and the coal oil for lights. I'm pleased."

"You should be." He looked at the sun. "Time for us to be moving back toward town. We still have those damn clues to work over."

Longarm sat bolt upright on the blanket. "I smelled that smell again today. I just didn't realize it. I remember where I was and who else was there."

"You did? Where was it? What was it?"

"Let me check for sure. Dress quickly and we'll hurry back to your house. I want to make one more check on those clues before we go and confront the embezzler and the man who killed Wally Johnson."

Chapter 16

All the way back to her small schoolmarm's house, Jennifer Walking Dove kept nagging at Longarm.

"Tell me who you think it is. Tell me what the smell was you remembered. Don't keep me in suspense this way."

Longarm grinned and walked faster. "First we need to check out those clues. We've got time, can't be more than three in the PM."

"You're not going to tell me."

"Reckon not. Not until I'm more sure than I am now."

"Beast!"

"True, but I'd appreciate that a lot more in the middle of playing slap and tickle, howsomeever I figure you really don't mean it. Think back over that last bunch of clues we looked at. Some of those figure into my new theory."

They were nearing the house now.

"Clues in the last bunch. I have them memorized: a small black briefcase of some kind, a grave marker, a buggy, a picture of a house, and a thermometer. Oh, and a bottle of cough syrup. Is that the way you remember them, Longarm?"

"Appears to be about it. I want to see them laid out and then do some rearranging of the whole batch. No—just the second two bunches."

They went upon the back porch, through the living room, and into the kitchen, where the clues were still spread on the table. Longarm went to work with them at once. He took the picture of the saw and the newborn baby from one group and put them in a row by themselves.

Then he picked out the black carrying case and the bottle of cough syrup and the thermometer and laid them in a line under the first two clues. Then he added the picture of the buggy, and at the bottom he put the grave marker.

He studied the setup for a while, then went back to the second set of clues and took the book and put it at the top of the row of pictures and drawings.

"There it is. Who is our killer?"

"That's nothing more than we had the first time. You just arranged them in different order."

"Oh, I forgot something." Longarm picked up a piece of paper that had "Smell" written on it and added it just above the grave marker. Then he took the two flat sticks and laid them beside the black case.

"Now, any more ideas?"

"I told you I'm not all that good with puzzles," Jennifer said. "I give up. Now tell me!"

Longarm chuckled. "It fooled me, too. The clues were all there, but I was fixing them wrong or interpreting what they meant in a contrary way.

"The rich man clue got us off to a bad start. Actually this man may still be rich, but he doesn't show it, so he didn't make our monied man group of suspects.

"But look at the rest of them. A book stands for an educated man, not a store owner or a cowhand. The newborn baby could mean anything, but one man in town has more to do with newborns than any other.

"Then there is the saw and the little black bag and the small sticks. Tools of the trade of someone in town. Any ideas yet?"

"You said rich men didn't count, so now we've got a whole town full of suspects," Jennifer protested.

"Not really. Look at those clues. Then add the cough syrup and the thermometer, more tools of the trade. And almost every one of these men has a buggy or uses one. When things go wrong in this profession, somebody often winds up under a grave marker."

"Oh, no! Now I see it. Those little sticks, they're like the ones a doctor uses to push down your tongue. The doctor's black bag, the saw for cutting bones, the thermometer, and the newborn baby. So it's the doctor, Doc Smith, after all!"

"That's what the clues point to. Even without the sticks and the smell."

"What was the smell? You didn't tell me that."

"That smell I caught a whiff of when the bushwhacker tried to kill me was familiar. I just couldn't tie it down. Then today when I took Deputy Elder into Doc Smith's office to get patched up, the nurse came and her hands reeked of the smell. It's a kind of disinfectant that doctors use to get everything sterile in their offices.

"The smell was what triggered my logic. Without tying that down, I might never have put all of these clues into the doctor solution."

"What are we going to do now, go to Sheriff Murdock?"

"With what? We have absolutely no evidence that would get past the district attorney and into court. We have nothing but Wally's list of clues and my nose. Not enough. We don't even know if the man has an alibi for that night.

"He's smart to have come this far. He must have taken part of the fifty thousand dollars and paid his way through medical school, then opened his practice here, and put the rest of his money away in his mattress."

"We have to shock him into admitting what he did," Jennifer said.

"Sure, how could we do that? He's been living with the embezzlement for eight years, and with the murder of Wally for the last week or so. What could make him admit it now?"

"Maybe I could."

"You? How?"

"Well, he knows Wally and I had been seeing each other. I could say that Wally told me why he was in town and that he had at last found the embezzler and was waiting for a federal lawman to arrest him."

"He'd just laugh at you. Your witness is dead. Your story is hearsay and wouldn't be admitted in court."

"I could also tell him that I'd been with Wally the night he was killed. I was in the shadows when Wally and Doc Smith had that last talk and agreed to meet out by the bridge."

"Only that meeting was set up with a note, not a meeting. We've got to think of something better."

"What if I told him that I'd been waiting to come see him about the diary that Wally kept? Wally wrote down everything concerning his investigation of the embezzler and it points directly to Dr. Smith. He's named and dates are given and all the conversations that they had."

"But there isn't such a diary."

"Dr. Smith doesn't know that."

"True. That could be dangerous. He's already killed once."

"Oh, I'll be careful. I'll tell him the diary's in a safe vault at the bank and I have the only key. Set it up so he'll try to find my key and get the diary—or I'll try to sell it to him."

"Might work," Longarm said. "Do you have a safe vault at the bank?"

"No."

"Then we'll need a key. I'll go talk to the banker, explain what we're doing. I'm sure that he'll go along with our plan. We'll get a key to an empty safe vault."

Jennifer smiled grimly. "At last I get a chance really to do something to help trap that killer. There's still time. I can go see the doctor this afternoon."

"I'll get right down to the bank before it closes and talk to James Leslie."

They hurried downtown together, and Longarm gave Jennifer's shoulder a squeeze for good luck before she continued on to the doctor's office.

He turned in at the bank just before it closed and asked to see Mr. Leslie.

The banker looked up, his face changing ever so slightly in recognition.

"Oh, yes, Marshal Long. Come in. What can I do for you today?"

Longarm told him briefly the problem, swore him to secrecy, and asked for a safe box key.

"We call them safe deposit boxes now," Leslie said. "It takes two keys to open them, one of ours here at the bank and one that's the customer's. Neither one of the keys alone will unlock the box."

"Perfect. I need to borrow a key, perhaps a demonstration one or one that's not in use for any of your boxes. We want to trap this man so he'll hang high."

Five minutes later, Longarm left the bank with safety deposit key #44 tucked in his pocket. He had arranged to meet Jennifer at the Larkspur Café on Main Street as soon as she had offered to sell the diary to Dr. Smith. She hadn't arrived when Longarm got to the eatery, so he had a cup of Arbuckle and sat down to wait.

After a half hour he got worried, went outside, and walked fifty feet each way in front of the café. The doctor's office was half a block north, and he could see the front door. On his tenth trip north to south in front of the café, he saw Jennifer come from the medic's office and walk his way. He slipped back inside and ordered coffee and jelly doughnuts for both of them.

The triumphant gleam in Jennifer Walking Dove's eyes when she marched into the café told Longarm that she had succeeded in laying the trap. She beamed as she sat down and sipped the coffee.

"Tell me about it."

"It worked! He bought the whole idea of the diary, said Wally looked to be that kind of a man, so damn meticulous. I told him it was all down in black and white and could hang him—unless he wanted to compensate me for it."

She sipped the coffee again.

"He was hanging on every word I said. I explained that Wally and I were courting, and he told me the whole story about Wally's father in Denver and the embezzlement and the loss and bankruptcy and how Wally's father died young.

"I told him about the note for the midnight meeting, the whole thing. I said I'd waited a week after Wally's death to get my own life back in order."

"He knew I'd been with you around town, and asked what you had figured out. I told him you had no evidence at all and said I'd been guiding you around, but you didn't know about the diary. Just some suspicions. I mentioned the clues that Wally left, too, that I had shown you, but told him the first ones pointed to a rich man. That interested him."

"What did you set up?"

"I said I'd give him the key to the safe box in exchange for twenty-five thousand dollars. The box is set up in my name, and I'll go with him tomorrow morning and get in it and give him the diary."

160

"But we don't have a real box or a diary."

"From the deadly look in his eyes, I don't think he'll wait until morning. I said that I am a cautious woman. The key is hidden in a special place and no one but me can find it. I also mentioned that I keep a shotgun beside my bed."

Longarm nodded. "I don't like the idea of using you as bait in the trap, but it was your idea. Too late to stop or change it, I reckon. Now there's only one thing to do. We get to your place and rig it. First we put a dummy in your bed and leave a lamp on, burning low. Then we'll lock the front and back doors and keep you as far away as possible. I'll be waiting inside the house for him to make his move."

"If he shoots the dummy and ransacks the house looking for the key, will that be enough to go to the sheriff?" Jennifer asked.

"It might. At least it will be enough to convince you and me that he's the killer."

"Why can't I shoot him down when he ransacks my house?"

"You could." Longarm looked at her seriously. "Have you ever killed another human being?"

Her brows shot up, and she covered her face with her hands. "No, and you're right. I don't think I could do it, even knowing what he did to Wally."

"So we play it my way."

They waited for darkness before they went into the school-marm's small house by the back door. She locked the front door, then they rigged a dummy made of rolled blankets in her bed and left the lamp burning low.

Out the back door, they walked to a farm wagon someone had parked a half block over. Jennifer had brought two comforters, and Longarm bundled her into them and told her that under no conditions should she move.

He ran back to the house and in the back door. He locked it with a skeleton key and pocketed it. These locks could be opened with almost any other skeleton key. If that didn't work, a good kick at the doorknob level usually sprang the door inward.

He found a chair, which he pushed against the far wall of the living room. From there he could see the kitchen and the bedroom. If Dr. Smith came in the front or the rear door, he would be in Longarm's sights.

161

Time passed.

Longarm got tired sitting on the hard chair and stood. He took out his watch and shielded a struck match. In the flare of the light he saw that it was nearly 10 P.M. The trap had been in place for more than three hours.

The next time Longarm checked his watch it was after 1 A.M. No takers.

He nearly fell off the chair when he want to sleep just before three in the morning.

At 5 A.M. a false dawn was starting. It was plain now that the doctor had decided not to try to get the key. Maybe he was going to pay.

In the lonely hours of the night, Longarm had come up with an alternate plan. He would confront the embezzler and make some kind of a threat or an offer. He wasn't sure yet.

At daylight, Jennifer came in, stiff and sore, cranky and looking as if she hadn't slept for a month. She boiled Arbuckle for them and combed her hair and changed clothes, and they both felt better.

"No meeting to trade the diary today," Longarm said. "Too risky. His plan would be to kill you, take the book, and keep his cash. Instead I'm going in and arrest him. Along the way I'll tell him our proof, including the diary and three eyewitnesses who saw him rent the buggy that afternoon, who saw him bring one back a little after 2 A.M. the morning of the killing, and a drifter who saw the murder scene out on the roadway."

"But you don't have those witnesses."

"He doesn't know that. I might force him into doing something stupid, like trying to bribe me or trying to kill me. Then we'd have him."

"Too dangerous," Jennifer said.

"That's what I get paid for. I'm going in as soon as I shave and have breakfast. I'll let him check over my arm wound, maybe have him change the bandage; then I'll spring my arrest plan on him."

"Too dangerous," Jennifer said, but not quite so forcefully.

Longarm walked into Dr. Smith's office that morning just after the white shade went up on his door. It was 9:15. There was no one else in the waiting room. The nurse, a big lady with a confident air, came in and took his name.

162

"Just to get the bullet hole checked and the bandage changed," Longarm said. She nodded and went out the door.

It was nearly five minutes later before she was back. She told Longarm to go into the first small room on the left. It was the one he had been in before, with a table, three lamps with mirrors on them to intensify the light, and a cabinet in which was assortment of medicines and instruments. He sat in the chair provided.

Dr. Smith hurried in, looking a little ruffled. The tall, thin man stared at Longarm a moment from intense brown eyes. Longarm again noticed the medic's slight limp as he walked.

"The arm, is it?"

"Yes sir, Dr. Smith. Been hurting a little lately. Figured you'd want to take another look at it."

Dr. Smith cut off the old bandage, but it didn't hurt the way it usually did. Longarm was surprised. This medic might actually know what he was doing. Dr. Smith brought a bottle with a green label and lathered some salve on the two holes in Longarm's flesh. Both holes had begun to heal nicely but would leave scar tissue.

"Looks fine. No reason why it should hurt. I'll put some special ointment on it I just got in. Supposed to hurry the healing process."

He looked at Longarm for a moment, then nodded. "The doctor I get it from in Boston says it's the absolute best there is. In your case I think it will work well." From a small bottle he dripped a dozen drops of the liquid on top of the ointment covering the bullet's exit wound, then wrapped the arm with a long roll of thin gauze until the bullet wound was tightly sealed and protected.

When he was done, Longarm thanked him, then stood up and flipped out his wallet and showed Dr. Smith the deputy United States marshal's badge with his name printed on it.

"Dr. Smith, I'm arresting you for the murder of Wallace Johnson in this county about a week ago. Specifics will be in the complaint. I'm charging you with meeting him on a pretext near Devil's Canyon Bridge and then and there slitting his throat, cutting both carotid arteries and allowing him to bleed to death. Then you shot his horse and pushed the buggy and horse over the side of the cliff into the canyon below. I'm charging you with first-degree murder."

Dr. Smith listened with almost no expression.

"Marshal, I don't have time for jokes. A man just came in with a cut finger and Mrs. Sebastian is about to have her baby this morning. If you'll excuse me."

Longarm took the handcuffs from the back of his belt. "I'm afraid not, Dr. Smith. You killed the boy and I can prove it. Jennifer Walking Dove showed me the diary her intended wrote in every day as he hunted you.

"Besides that I have reliable witnesses who can put you at the scene of the crime. We have motive, and opportunity. He would have exposed you as a wanted felon and ruined your practice here and sent you back to Denver for a trial and a sure conviction."

Chapter 17

Dr. Smith stood beside his cabinet of medicines with shock, then anger, spreading over his face.

"I don't know what you're talking about. I've never been in Denver. I come from Chicago. My parents had money and put me through medical school. Then I came here to practice. Ask anyone in town about my work. I've been saving lives here for five years."

Longarm nodded. "True, Dr. Smith, until you took one life that threatened you. No matter what you say, we have enough evidence to arrest you for murder. The district attorney agrees, and the grand jury will be quick to indict you as well."

Dr. Smith produced a thin smile. "I would guess that being the kind of a man you are, you probably have gathered most of the evidence yourself. That being the situation, your case against me may crumble and die before you know it. How are you feeling, Marshal Long?"

"I feel fine." Then all of a sudden, he didn't. His head started pounding; then he had to lean against the wall to catch his balance.

"Yes, the balance goes first. It's a rather painless death, though."

"The damn bandage and those drops. What did you drip on my wound?" Longarm shouted. He ripped at the tape and began unwinding the gauze strips from around his upper left arm.

"You put something in that salve. What was it?"

Dr. Smith looked more confident now. "The poison? It's a derivative of curare, the deadly South American poison the Indians down there use to tip their arrows. Actually it's a dried extract of the *Strychnos toxifera* vine in solution. Often kills within minutes."

Longarm kept unwrapping the bandages. They were wet now with the medicine and the poison.

"My only uncertainty was how long it would take the poison to work through the salve," Dr. Smith said. "But I see it's starting to take hold."

By then Longarm had the wound open. He grabbed a towel and dug all of the medicine and the liquid poison away from the wound. Then he reeled toward the doctor. His right hand stabbed for the cross-draw rig but missed it.

"Well now, the old rattler still has some sting left in him. I might as well administer a second dose of the curare." The doctor reached to the shelf and took down the same small vial he had used before. He dipped the blade of one of his scalpels into the purplish fluid. He walked slowly toward Longarm.

"You might as well just relax. This will all be over in a minute or two. I'll cut into a mass where the poison will be absorbed by the tissue itself and not washed into the blood. Yes, best method."

Longarm saw the man in the long white coat coming toward him. He backed away. His arms and legs weren't working right. He'd never felt so light-headed before in his life. He tried to swing one arm, but it fell far short of the doctor.

He tried to draw his six-gun. He moved his right hand slowly around his belt and found the butt of his Colt .44-40. Gently he drew it out and tried to cock the hammer. His thumb didn't work right.

The doctor was closer now.

"Oh my, you did get to your gun. Hate the things. Always use a knife. Like this."

He made a swipe at Longarm with the poison-wet blade, but Longarm stumbled backward and fell against an examining table. The sudden movement made the doctor miss with the deadly scalpel by half an inch.

166

Longarm concentrated with every thought in his mind, ordering his right thumb to cock the hammer. The doctor recovered from his miss and advanced again, this time from only three feet away.

Longarm tried to swing the Colt up to aim at the white coat. He turned the weapon in his strong right hand, which now felt like a wet noodle. He brought up his left hand as well and held the six-gun with both. His left finger doubled on the trigger and he fired. The round tore into the floorboards at the doctor's feet.

"I'm not afraid of guns, Longarm, just never use them. Now relax and this will be all over in a minute."

Someone pounded on the locked examining-room door.

"Doctor?" the nurse called.

"It's all right, Phyllis. The marshal was just demonstrating to me how a revolver works. Nothing to worry about."

The interruption allowed Longarm to lift the heavy Colt higher, and just as Dr. Smith pushed out his hand to give the deadly cut, Longarm fired again. The weapon had risen only to the thigh level, but the big slug jolted into the doctor's left leg, spun him around, and sprawled him onto the floor six feet away.

"Bastard!" Dr. Smith bellowed.

Longarm's eyes were misted now, and his movements slow, but he held the weapon in both hands and took slow, deliberate steps to where the medic lay. Through foggy eyes, Longarm saw what had happened. The bullet hadn't killed the man where it hit him in the left thigh, but the razor-blade-sharp scalpel with the load of deadly curare poison had dropped from the doctor's hand when he fell, and the lethal point had penetrated to the hilt in the middle of Dr. Smith's throat.

Longarm blinked furiously so he could see better. He held the six-gun and slowly knelt beside the doctor. Already the medic's eyes were glazed. He tried to lift one hand.

"Right into the bloodstream. Damn. I didn't figure it would go this way. Damn. Rest of the money is in the medical storage closet. Tell old man Johnson that I'm sorry." His eyes closed, his head turned slowly to the side, and Longarm heard a final rush of unused air out of the dead man's lungs.

The pounding came on the door again. Longarm tried to talk, but he couldn't. He crawled over on his hands and knees and with great effort opened the door.

Nurse Phyllis stood there. She bleated in terror and ran to the doctor. She saw the scalpel and started to pull it out.

"Leave it there," Longarm said in a whisper. "I'm a deputy U.S. marshal and Dr. Smith is a killer. He used curare poison on my wound. Half-dead myself. Any way you can wash off the poison?"

The nurse jumped up, looked over several bottles, and then brought down one and poured the white liquid in it over his wound. She moved his arm over the sink and kept dousing the wound with the fluid. The smell that hit Longarm's nose made him grin. It was the same antiseptic odor he'd been chasing for so long. She followed that with a hot-water scrub, then more of the whitish fluid.

The fog was still there, dulling his whole nervous system, putting it on half speed. He knew what the woman was doing, but nothing else made much sense. He felt as if he were floating in a dense sea of vapor, and for the life of him, he really didn't care if he ever came out of it. In a way it was peaceful there, relaxing, no worries.

A few minutes later he saw someone else at the door. A small girl with black bangs ... Jennifer. She ran to him and talked to the nurse, but Longarm couldn't understand the words.

Sometime later he was aware that he was being moved. Two men and Jennifer picked him up and took him to another room, where they lowered him onto a bed. Then the lights faded and he wasn't sure where he was. Slowly, ever so slowly, the whole room turned to black.

For just a second, Longarm wondered if this was what death was like.

Two days later, he felt a cold cloth on his forehead. Slowly he opened his eyes. The room was so bright he snapped his eyes shut. He heard a small cry of joy by his side. That had to be an angel or Jennifer. He tried his slitted eyes again, and this time he could manage the shaded light in the room.

Longarm turned his head and saw Jennifer's tear-stained face.

"Thank God you're all right!" She bent and kissed his cheek, and new tears seeped from her eyes.

"Feel like I went through a cotton gin, twice," Longarm said. His speech was slow; his lips felt thick and his words hard to understand.

"Aftereffects. Nurse Phyllis told us all about it. Dr. Smith had been experimenting with the poison on stray dogs to see if low doses of it could be beneficial in any way. The dogs came around slowly, too, she said.

"Nurse Phyllis has been a marvel, a wonder. She had no idea who Dr. Smith was, or that he killed Wally. Dr. Smith . . . he . . . he died, you know."

"Figured," Longarm said with satisfaction.

"You shot him in the leg. Was that when he dropped the scalpel and the bottle of poison?"

"Yes. The blade was meant for me." His words were better now. He swallowed and asked for some water, and after drinking a little, he went on. "He wanted to finish me off." Longarm looked at the beautiful Indian girl and smiled. "Hey, I think I'm going to recover."

"You will, but it will take two weeks. That's the word of a doctor in Santa Fe who sent a message when he heard about the curare poisoning. I've arranged to take you by buggy to my place. I have nothing else to do until September when school opens."

"First we need to talk to Sheriff Murdock." His voice was almost back to normal.

"He's in the hall waiting. Nurse said you should be nearly over the effects of the poison in about two days. But I'm telling everyone two weeks. You feel ready to talk to the sheriff now?"

"Ayuh."

Sheriff Murdock came into the room, hat in hand. His worried expression changed when he saw Longarm half sitting up.

"Good to see you alive, Longarm."

"Good to be nearly alive."

"Schoolmarm here filled me in on everything 'cepting what happened after you went to see the doc."

"I accused him, told him we had evidence we didn't really have, including a diary. He doped my wound with curare as he rebandaged it. Took some time to get through the salve and start affecting me. I turned all groggy, but I got in one

169

shot. He slammed backward, and the scalpel with the curare on it, intended to finish me, fell and jammed in his throat. He must have died in a minute or two."

"That's it?"

"Yep. Case closed. Two cases closed. Now, could you send a wire to my chief for me? Tell him what he needs to know about the embezzler, now in hell by his own hand. Also tell him about the curare and that the nurse says it'll take me two weeks to recuperate enough to get back to Denver. Also there's some of the stolen cash to recover."

"I'll get a message on the evening stage to Santa Fe, and it'll get wired directly by night clerk. Anything else?"

"Not that I got hold of right now."

"Where will you be recuperating?"

"I've been hired on to nurse Mr. Long until he's well enough to travel," Jennifer said from the doorway. "Part of my responsibility. I mean, I nagged him into trying to find Wally's killer."

Sheriff Murdock chuckled. "Reckon we don't need to put that in the official report. I'll get this off pronto. Oh, when you're up to it, I'll need a signed statement from you about how Dr. Smith died. Also we need to put an advertisement in the Santa Fe newspaper for a new sawbones up here." The lawman stood, turned his hat in his hands once, smiled at Jennifer, and then eased out the door.

Longarm looked up at the small Pueblo Indian girl, who pushed as close to the bed as she could get.

"You really meant that about nursing me for a time?"

"Try and stop me."

"Oh, well, it might not be all that terrible come to think of it. You still make apple pie?"

"I do."

"You can fetch cold beer from one of the taverns and hunt around until you find some Gibson's Choice rye whiskey? Think you can do that?"

"I'm sure I can find some here or in Santa Fe."

"You'd go to all that trouble?"

"You bet. You tracked down Wally's killer when the clues were there right in front of my face all the time and I couldn't make the connection. If Doc Smith had shown off some of his stolen money, we'd have had an easier time of it."

"Ayuh, both of us. Oh, can you bring the nurse in here?"

Jennifer brought Phyllis in.

"Yes, Mr. Long. What can I do for you?"

"Take a good look in back of the medical storage closet and see what you find. I'd guess you'll dig out something like cash of the realm. A lot of that cash should still have Denver bank bands around it."

Jennifer went along on the search and came back in half an hour with a carpetbag stuffed with federal bank notes. The nurse looked on and shook her head.

"Dozens of times I asked the doctor for some new instrument or equipment that would help our patients. He put me off, saying we didn't have the money to buy it. Glory, and here we was sitting on all this cash."

"Stolen money, Phyllis," Jennifer said. "He couldn't afford to show any unusual amount of money or folks might have been suspicious. Longarm would have been, so the doc played it safe."

"Let's count the currency," Longarm commanded. "Don't break the bank bands. There should be a figure on the outside of each one. We'll list those figures, then tally them up. Oh, first run over and bring a sheriff's deputy here to help us and to be a witness."

It took the better part of two hours, and when they were done they had a total of $34,489.

"For an embezzler, Doc Smith lived frugally on his stolen cash," Longarm said. The deputy signed a receipt for the money and called for a second deputy to help him witness it and take it over to the sheriff's safe.

The stolen loot would be held until it was requested that it be returned to Denver for proper distribution.

"Some of the folks who lost everything in that bank failure will get a little of their money back," Longarm said. "Hey, I'm tired. Get out of here, you guys, so I can have a nap. We'll talk tomorrow. When do I move?"

Jennifer grinned at him and started to close the door.

"Jen, you don't have to go. I've got room beside me here in bed if you want to take a small nap, too."

"Great idea," she said. She curled up beside him, clothes and all. "We have two whole weeks to get you back into top form before I let you go back to Denver. I know how you

171

hate being out of your marshal-lawman kind of action. As far as I'm concerned, I'd just as soon you stay right here."

She reached over and kissed his cheek and knew it wouldn't be more than a day or two before Longarm would be as frisky and sexy as ever.

Jennifer Walking Dove, Pueblo Indian schoolmarm of the Taos Town School, could hardly wait.

Watch for

LONGARM AND THE NEVADA SWINDLE

171st in the exciting LONGARM series from Jove

Coming in March!

SPECIAL PREVIEW!

Giles Tippette, America's new star of the classic western, brings to life the adventures of an outlaw gone straight—who's got everything at stake facing a no-account gambler . . .

Dead Man's Poker

By the acclaimed author of *Gunpoint, Sixkiller,* and *Hard Rock.*

Here is a special excerpt from this authentic new western—available from Jove Books . . .

I was hurt, though how badly I didn't know. Some three hours earlier I'd been shot, the ball taking me in the left side of the chest about midway up my rib cage. I didn't know if the slug had broken a rib or just passed between two of them as it exited my back. I'd been in Galveston, trying to collect a gambling debt, when, like a fool kid, I'd walked into a setup that I'd ordinarily have seen coming from the top of a tree stump. I was angry that I hadn't collected the debt, I was more than angry that I'd been shot, but I was furious at myself for having been suckered in such a fashion. I figured if it ever got around that Wilson Young had been gotten that easy, all of the old enemies I'd made through the years would start coming out of the woodwork to pick over the carcass.

But, in a way, I was lucky. By rights I should have been killed outright, facing three of them as I had and having nothing to put me on the alert. They'd had guns in their hands by the time I realized it wasn't money I was going to get, but lead.

Now I was rattling along on a train an hour out of Galveston, headed for San Antonio. It had been lucky, me catching that train just as it was pulling out. Except for that, there was an excellent chance that I would have been incarcerated in Galveston and looking at more trouble than I'd been in in a long time. After the shooting I'd managed to get away from the office where the trouble had happened and make my way toward the depot. I'd been wearing a frock coat of a good quality linen when I'd sat down with Phil Sharp to discuss the money he owed me. Because it was a hot day, I took the coat off and laid it over the arm of the chair I was sitting in. When the shooting was over, I grabbed the coat and the little valise I was carrying and ducked and dodged my way through alleyways and side streets. I came up from the border on the train so, of course, I didn't have a horse with me.

But I did have a change of clothes, having expected to be overnight in Galveston. In an alley I took off my bloody shirt, inspected the wound in my chest, and then wrapped the shirt around me, hoping to keep the blood from showing. Then I put on a clean shirt that fortunately was dark and not white like the one I'd been shot in. After that I donned my frock coat, picked up my valise, and made my way to the train station. I did not know if the law was looking for me or not, but I waited until the train was ready to pull out before I boarded it. I had a round-trip ticket so there'd been no need for me to go inside the depot.

I knew I was bleeding, but I didn't know how long it would be before the blood seeped through my makeshift bandage and then through my shirt and finally showed on my coat.

All I knew was that I was hurting and hurting bad and that I was losing blood to the point where I was beginning to feel faint. It was a six-hour ride to San Antonio, and I was not at all sure I could last that long. Even if the blood didn't seep through enough to call it to someone's attention, I might well pass out. But I didn't have many options. There were few stops between Galveston and San Antonio, it being a kind of a spur line, and what there were would be small towns that most likely wouldn't even have a doctor. I could get off in one and lay up in a hotel until I got better, but that didn't much appeal to me. I wanted to know how bad I was hurt, and the only way I was going to know that was to hang on until I could get to some good medical attention in San Antone.

I was Wilson Young, and in that year of 1896, I was thirty-two years old. For fourteen of those years, beginning when I was not quite fifteen, I had been a robber. I'd robbed banks, I'd robbed money shipments, I'd robbed high-stakes poker games, I'd robbed rich people carrying more cash than they ought to have been, but mostly I'd robbed banks. But then about four years past, I'd left the owlhoot trail and set out to become a citizen that did not constantly have to be on the lookout for the law. Through the years I'd lost a lot of friends and a lot of members of what the newspapers had chosen to call my "gang"—the Texas Bank Robbing Gang in one headline.

I'd even lost a wife, a woman I'd taken out of a whorehouse in the very same town I was now fleeing from. But Mariane hadn't been a whore at heart; she'd just been kind of briefly and unwillingly forced into it in much the same way I'd taken up robbing banks.

I had been making progress in my attempt to achieve a certain amount of respectability. At first I'd set up on the Mexican side of the border, making occasional forays into Texas to sort of test the waters. Then, as a few years passed and certain amounts of money found their way into the proper hands, I was slowly able to make my way around Texas. I had not been given a pardon by the governor, but emissaries of his had indicated that the state of Texas was happy to have no further trouble with Wilson Young and that the past could be forgotten so long as I did nothing to revive it.

And now had come this trouble. The right or wrong of my position would have nothing to do with it. I was still Wilson Young, and if I was in a place where guns were firing and men were being shot, the prevailing attitude was going to be that it was my doing.

So it wasn't only the wound that was troubling me greatly; it was also the worry about the aftermath of what had begun as a peaceful and lawful business trip. If I didn't die from my wound, there was every chance that I would become a wanted man again, and there would go the new life I had built for myself. And not only that life of peace and legality, but also a great deal of money that I had put into a business in Del Rio, Texas, right along the banks of the Rio Grande. Down there, a stone's throw from Mexico, I owned the most high-class saloon and gambling emporium and whorehouse as there was to be found in Texas. I had at first thought to put it on the Mexican side of the river, but the *mordida,* the bribes, that the officials would have taken convinced me to build it

179

in Texas, where the local law was not quite so greedy. But now, if trouble were to come from this shooting, I'd have to be in Mexico, and my business would be in Texas. It might have been only a stone's throw away, but for me, it might just as well have been a thousand miles. And I'd sunk damn near every cent I had in the place.

My side was beginning to hurt worse with every mile. I supposed it was my wound, but the train was rattling around and swaying back and forth like it was running on crooked rails. I was in the last car before the caboose, and every time we rounded a curve, the car would rock back and forth like it was fixing to quit the tracks and take off across the prairie. Fortunately, the train wasn't very crowded and I had a seat to myself. I was sort of sitting in the middle of the double cushion and leaning to my right against the wall of the car. It seemed to make my side rest easier to stretch it out like that. My valise was at my feet, and with a little effort, I bent down and fumbled it open with my right hand. Since my wound had begun to stiffen up, my left arm had become practically useless—to use it would almost put tears in my eyes.

I had a bottle of whiskey in my valise, and I fumbled it out, pulled the cork with my teeth and then had a hard pull. There was a spinsterish middle-aged lady sitting right across the aisle from me, and she give me such a look of disapproval that I thought for a second that she was going to call the conductor and make a commotion. As best I could, I got the cork back in the bottle and then hid it out of sight between my right side and the wall of the car.

Outside, the terrain was rolling past. It was the coastal prairie of south Texas, acres and acres of flat, rolling plains that grew the best grazing grass in the state. It would stay that way until the train switched tracks and turned west for San Antonio. But that was another two hours away. My plan was to get myself fixed up in San Antone and then head out for Del Rio and the Mexican side of the border just as fast as I could. From there I'd try and find out just what sort of trouble I was in.

That was, if I lived that long.

With my right hand I pulled back the left side of my coat, lifting it gently, and looked underneath. I could see just the beginning of a stain on the dark blue shirt I'd changed into.

Soon it would soak through my coat and someone would notice it. I had a handkerchief in my pocket, and I got that out and slipped it inside my shirt, just under the stain. I had no way of holding it there, but so long as I kept still, it would stay in place.

Of course I didn't know what was happening at my back. For all I knew the blood had already seeped through and stained my coat. That was all right so long as my back was against the seat, but it would be obvious as soon as I got up. I just had to hope there would be no interested people once I got to San Antone and tried to find a doctor.

I knew the bullet had come out my back. I knew it because I'd felt around and located the exit hole while I'd been hiding in the alley, using one shirt for a bandage and the other for a sop. Of course the hole in my back was bigger than the entrance hole the bullet had made. It was always that way, especially if a bullet hit something hard like a bone and went to tumbling or flattened out. I could have stuck my thumb in the hole in my back.

About the only good thing I could find to feel hopeful about was the angle of the shot. The bullet had gone in very near the bottom of my ribs and about six inches from my left side. But it had come out about only three or four inches from my side. That meant there was a pretty good chance that it had missed most of the vital stuff and such that a body has got inside itself. I knew it hadn't nicked my lungs because I was breathing fine. But there is a whole bunch of other stuff inside a man that a bullet ain't going to do a bit of good. I figured it had cracked a rib for sure because it hurt to breathe deep, but that didn't even necessarily have to be so. It was hurting so bad anyway that I near about couldn't separate the different kinds of hurt.

A more unlikely man than Phil Sharp to give me my seventh gunshot wound I could not have imagined. I had ended my career on the owlhoot trail with my body having lived through six gunshots. That, as far as I was concerned, had been a-plenty. By rights I should have been dead, and there had been times when I had been given up for dead. But once off the outlaw path I'd thought my days of having my blood spilt were over. Six was enough.

And then Phil Sharp had given me my seventh. As a gambler I didn't like the number. There was nothing lucky about it that

I could see, and I figured that anything that wasn't lucky had to be unlucky.

Part of my bad luck was because I *was* Wilson Young. Even though I'd been retired for several years, I was still, strictly speaking, a wanted man. And if anybody had cause to take interest in my condition, it might mean law—and law would mean trouble.

For that matter Phil Sharp and the three men he'd had with him might have thought they could shoot me without fear of a murder charge because of the very fact of my past and my uncertain position with regard to the law, both local and through the state. Hell, for all I knew some of those rewards that had been posted on my head might still be lying around waiting for someone to claim them. It hadn't been so many years past that my name and my likeness had been on Wanted posters in every sheriff's office in every county in Texas.

I had gone to see Phil Sharp because he'd left my gambling house owing me better than twenty thousand dollars. I didn't, as an ordinary matter, advance credit at the gaming tables, but Sharp had been a good customer in the past and I knew him to be a well-to-do man. He owned a string of warehouses along the docks in Galveston, which was the biggest port in Texas. The debt had been about a month old when I decided to go and see him. When he'd left Del Rio, he'd promised to wire me the money as soon as he was home, but it had never come. Letters and telegrams jogging his memory had done no good, so I'd decided to call on him in person. It wasn't just the twenty thousand; there was also the matter that it ain't good policy for a man running a casino and cathouse to let word get around that he's careless about money owed him. And in that respect I was still the Wilson Young it was best not to get too chancy with. Sharp knew my reputation and I did not figure to have any trouble with him. If he didn't have the twenty thousand handy, I figured we could come to some sort of agreement as to how he could pay it off. I had wired him before I left Del Rio that I was planning a trip to Houston and was going to look in on him in Galveston. He'd wired back that he'd be expecting me.

I saw him in his office in the front of one of the warehouses he owned down along the waterfront. He was behind his desk when I was shown in, getting up to shake hands with me. He was dressed like he usually was, in an expensive suit with a shiny vest and a big silk tie. Sharp himself was a little round man in his forties with a kind of baby face and a look that promised you could trust him with your virgin sister. Except I'd seen him without the suit and vest, chasing one of my girls down the hall at four o'clock in the morning with a bottle of whiskey in one hand and the handle to his hoe in the other. I'd also seen him at the poker table with sweat pouring off his face as he tried to make a straight beat a full house. It hadn't then and it probably never would.

He acted all surprised that I hadn't gotten my money, claiming he'd mailed it to me no less than a week ago. He said, "I got to apologize for the delay, but I had to use most of my ready cash on some shipments to England. Just let me step in the next room and look at my canceled checks. I'd almost swear I saw it just the other day. Endorsed by you."

Like I said, he looked like a man that might shoot you full of holes in a business deal, but not the sort of man who could use or would use a gun.

He got up from his desk and went to a door at the back, just to my right. I took off my coat and laid it over the arm of the chair, it being warm in the office. I was sitting kind of forward on the chair, feeling a little uneasy for some reason. It was that, but it was mainly the way Sharp opened the back door that probably saved my life. When you're going through a door, you pull it to you and step to your left, toward the opening, so as to pass through. But Sharp pulled open the door and then stepped back. In that instant, I slid out of the chair I was sitting in and down to my knees. As I did, three men with hoods pulled over their heads came through the door with pistols in their hands. Their first volley would have killed me if I'd still been sitting in the chair. But they fired at where I'd been, and by the time they could cock their pistols for another round, I had my revolver in my hand and was firing. They never got off another shot; all three went down under my rapid-fire volley.

Then I became aware that Phil Sharp was still in the room, just by the open door. I was about to swing my revolver around on him when I saw a little gun in his hand. He fired, once, and hit me in the chest. I knew it was a low-caliber gun because the blow of the slug just twitched at my side, not even knocking me off balance.

183

But it surprised me so that it gave Sharp time to cut through the open door and disappear into the blackness of the warehouse. I fired one shot after him, knowing it was in vain, and then pulled the trigger on an empty chamber.

I had not brought any extra cartridges with me. In the second I stood there with an empty gun, I couldn't remember why I hadn't brought any extras, but the fact was that I was standing there, wounded, with what amounted to a useless piece of iron in my fist. As quick as I could, expecting people to suddenly come bursting in the door, I got over to where the three men were lying on the floor and began to check their pistols to see if they fired the same caliber ammunition I did. But I was out of luck. My revolver took a .40-caliber shell; all three of the hooded men were carrying .44-caliber pistols.

Two of the men were dead, but one of them was still alive. I didn't have time to mess with him, but I turned him over so he could hear me good and said, "Tell Phil Sharp I ain't through with him. Nor your bunch either."

Then I got out of there and started making my way for the train depot. At first the wound bothered me hardly at all. In fact at first I thought I'd just been grazed. But then, once outside, I saw the blood spreading all over the front of my shirt and I knew that I was indeed hit. I figured I'd been shot by nothing heavier than a .32-caliber revolver but a .32 can kill you just as quick as a cannon if it hits you in the right place.

LONGARM

Explore the exciting Old West with
one of the men who made it wild!

If you enjoyed this book, subscribe now and get...

TWO FREE

A $7.00 VALUE–

If you would like to read more of the very best, most exciting, adventurous, action-packed Westerns being published today, you'll want to subscribe to True Value's Western Home Subscription Service.

Each month the editors of True Value will select the 6 very best Westerns from America's leading publishers for special readers like you. You'll be able to preview these new titles as soon as they are published, *FREE* for ten days with no obligation!

TWO FREE BOOKS

When you subscribe, we'll send you your first month's shipment of the newest and best 6 Westerns for you to preview. With your first shipment, two of these books will be yours as our introductory gift to you absolutely *FREE* (a $7.00 value), regardless of what you decide to do. If

you like them, as much as we think you will, keep all six books but pay for just 4 at the low subscriber rate of just $2.75 each. If you decide to return them, keep 2 of the titles as our gift. No obligation.

Special Subscriber Savings

When you become a True Value subscriber you'll save money several ways. First, all regular monthly selections will be billed at the low subscriber price of just $2.75 each. That's at least a savings of $4.50 each month below the publishers price. Second, there is never any shipping, handling or other hidden charges—*Free home delivery*. What's more there is no minimum number of books you must buy, you may return any selection for full credit and you can cancel your subscription at any time. A TRUE VALUE!

A special offer for people who enjoy reading the best Westerns published today.

WESTERNS!

NO OBLIGATION

Mail the coupon below

To start your subscription and receive 2 FREE WESTERNS, fill out the coupon below and mail it today. We'll send your first shipment which includes 2 FREE BOOKS as soon as we receive it.

J.R. ROBERTS
THE
GUNSMITH